T0083496

Karolinum Press

MODERN CZECH CLASSICS

Jaroslav Kvapil
Rusalka
A Lyrical Fairy Tale in Three Acts

Bilingual Edition
Translation from the Czech by Patrick John Corness
Afterword by Geoffrey Chew

KAROLINUM PRESS 2020

KAROLINUM PRESS
Karolinum Press is a publishing department
of Charles University
Ovocný trh 5/560, 116 36 Prague 1
Czech Republic
www.karolinum.cz

Jaroslav Kvapil's *Rusalka: Lyrická pohádka o třech dějstvích* formed
the libretto for Antonín Dvořák's opera, which premiered
31 March 1901 in Prague's National Theatre. The libretto was first
published in 1901 by F. Topič. The Czech text that appears in this
edition comes from 1948's *Souborné dílo Jaroslava Kvapila o čtyřech
svazcích.* Vol. 3, *Divadlo Jaroslava Kvapila* (Prague: Dr Václav Tomsa).

Cataloguing-in-Publication Data is available from the National Library
of the Czech Republic

ISBN 978-80-246-4381-6 (pb)
ISBN 978-80-246-4705-0 (epub)
ISBN 978-80-246-4704-3 (mobi)
ISBN 978-80-246-4700-5 (pdf)

Jaroslav Kvapil (1868–1950) was a Czech poet, playwright, translator, and theatre director.

Born in the Bohemian town of Chudenice, when it was still part of the Austro-Hungarian Empire, he was sent to secondary school in Plzeň and moved to Prague to study at Charles University. He studied medicine for a year before switching to philology and then law. When he left university, he went to work as a journalist. As a young man, he came to the attention of Prague's literary circles primarily for his poetry, which incorporated symbolist and Parnassian influences.

Inspired by his relationship with the actress Hana Kubešová, Kvapil began to focus more on theatrical work, writing scripts, translating plays, and directing. In 1900, he joined the Czech National Theatre as a dramaturg; he became the chief director in 1906 and served as the head of dramaturgy between 1911–1918. In his eighteen years with the National Theatre, he brought Czech drama into the mainstream of European theatre—staging plays by leading European playwrights, such as Ibsen and Chekhov. Kvapil's work is remarkable in its reflections of emerging artistic movements, shifting from symbolism to realism and naturalism.

During the First World War, Kvapil became a leading voice calling for Czechoslovak independence. When the war ended, Kvapil served three years as the minister of education and culture, before becoming the artistic director of Prague's Vinohrady Theatre.

A strong proponent of democracy, Kvapil was arrested by the Gestapo in 1944 and imprisoned until the end of World War II. When the Communists took power in 1948, Kvapil resisted pressure to support the new regime.

Today, Jaroslav Kvapil is best known for writing the libretto for Antonín Dvořák's *Rusalka*. A truly European work, it draws inspiration from Hans Christian Andersen's "Little Mermaid," as well as the Czech fairy tales of Karel Jaromír Erben.

OSOBY

Lesní žínka
Druhá žínka
Třetí žínka
Vodník (Hastrman, Hastrmánek)
Rusalka
Rusalky

Ježibaba

Lovec
Princ
Hajný
Kuchtík

Cizí kněžna

CHARACTERS

Wood Nymph
Second Wood Nymph
Third Wood Nymph
Spirit of the Lake (Water Spirit)
Rusalka (Water Nymph)
Water Nymphs

Ježibaba (Forest Witch)

Huntsman
Prince
Gamekeeper
Kitchen Hand

Foreign Princess

*Palouk na pokraji jezera. Kolkolem lesy, v nich na břehu jezera
chalupa čarodějnice Ježibaby.*

ACT ONE

A glade on the shore of a lake, surrounded by forest. Among the trees at the lakeside stands the cottage of the witch Ježibaba.

TŘI LESNÍ ŽÍNKY – *tančí na palouku*:
Hou, hou, hou,
stojí měsíc nad vodou!
Zvědavě se v hloubku dívá,
po kameni ke dnu splývá,
hastrmánek hlavou kývá,
hou, hou, hou,
starou hlavou zelenou.

Hou, hou, hou,
kdo to chodí nocí tou?
Hastrmánku, měsíc stoupá,
už se tobě v okně houpá,
za chvíli se k tobě vloupá,
hou, hou, hou,
ve tvou síňku stříbrnou!

Hou, hou, hou,
měsíc bloudí nad vodou![1]
Po jezeře tančí vánek,
probudil se hastrmánek,
hastrmánek, tatrmánek,
hou, hou, hou,
bublinky už ze dna jdou.

Vodník se vynoří z jezera a mne si oči.

LESNÍ ŽÍNKY:
Hou, hou, hou,
hastrmánek nad vodou!
Hastrmánek chce se ženit,
která z vás chce vodu pěnit,

1) In an earlier edition: *bloudí lučinou*

THREE WOOD NYMPHS – *dancing in the glade*:
Hey, hey, ho –
the moon lights up the lake below.
She peers right down into the deep,
and glides across the stony bed.
The Water Spirit is asleep –
hey, hey, ho –
nodding away, Old Green Head.

Hey, hey, ho –
who goes there at dead of night?
Water Spirit, the moon shines bright,
she's bobbing at your window, so
quite soon inside your home she'll steal –
hey, hey, ho –
upon your silver den she'll call –

Hey, hey, ho –
the roaming moon lights up the lake.
A gentle breeze is dancing there.
The Water Spirit is awake,
Water Spirit – it's Old Green Hair –
hey, hey, ho –
blowing bubbles from below!

   *Spirit of the Lake emerges above the surface
   of the lake, rubbing his eyes.*

WOOD NYMPHS:
Hey, hey, ho –
Here's Water Spirit from below!
Water Spirit wants a wife;
which one of you will cause some strife,

dědka česat, ложе změnit,
hou, hou, hou,
s babkou hastrmanovou?

VODNÍK:
I, pěkně vítám z lesa k jezeru!
Jakž, je tam smutno bujným slečinkám?
Mám dole na dně samu nádheru
a zlatých rybek na pytle tam mám;
rákosím se kmitnu,
ruku svou jen napnu,
po slečince chňapnu,
za nožky ji chytnu,
stáhnu si ji k nám!
Lapá po lesních žínkách.

LESNÍ ŽÍNKY:
Hastrmánku, heja hej,
tedy si nás nachytej!
Kterou chytíš, mužíčku,
dá ti pěknou hubičku!
Ale žena, hahaha,
hastrmánku, hahaha,
za uši ti vytahá!
Rozutekou se.

VODNÍK:
Uličnická havěť! Kterak zbrkle pádí!
Horem dolem polem – inu, mládí, mládí!

RUSALKA – *vynoří se z jezera*:
Hastrmánku tatíčku!

brush the hair on the old man's head –
hey, hey, ho –
usurp the Old Green Woman's bed?

SPIRIT OF THE LAKE:
You're welcome on our shore, wood sprites!
If you lively girls feel bored out there,
down here, you know, I've nothing but delights.
I've golden fish galore, there's bags to spare;
through rushes I'll flit,
just reach out a bit,
snatch a damsel's toe.
catch her leg like so,
draw her down below.
 He tries to catch the wood nymphs.

WOOD NYMPHS:
Water Spirit, ha, ha, ha!
come on, catch us if you can!
The one you catch, my dear man,
she will kiss you, ha, ha, ha!
But then your wife, ooh la la!
old Water Spirit, ha, ha, ha!
she'll box your ears, ha, ha, ha!
 They scatter.

SPIRIT OF THE LAKE:
Oh, what a cheeky lot! They always rush headlong
up hill, down dale – ah well, they're young, so young!

RUSALKA – *surfacing in the lake*:
Water Spirit, father dear!

VODNÍK:
Kýho šlaka, dítě,
snad mi tady v měsíčku
nesušíš mé sítě?

RUSALKA:
Hastrmánku tatíčku,
než se vody zpění,
sečkej se mnou chviličku,
ať mi smutno není!

VODNÍK:
I vida, smutno!

RUSALKA:
Všechno řeknu ti!

VODNÍK:
A dole taky?

RUSALKA:
Smutno k zalknutí!

VODNÍK:
Dole, kde je samý rej?
Není možná – povídej!

RUSALKA:
Chtěla bych od vás, hlubin těch se zbýti,
člověkem být a v zlatém slunci žíti!

VODNÍK:
Mohu-liž věřit vlastním uším svým?
Člověkem býti? Tvorem smrtelným?

SPIRIT OF THE LAKE:
Oh goodness me, my child,
are you, in this moonlight clear,
seeing my nets get dried?

RUSALKA:
Water Spirit, father dear,
until the water starts to foam,
bide with me a while, stay near,
console me in my gloom.

SPIRIT OF THE LAKE:
You're sad, I see!

RUSALKA:
I'll tell you what ails me.

SPIRIT OF THE LAKE:
At home you aren't happy?

RUSALKA:
So sad it stifles me!

SPIRIT OF THE LAKE:
Below we're such a joyful throng.
This can't be true. Tell me what's wrong.

RUSALKA:
Your depths down here I want to shun
to be a human, living in the sun.

SPIRIT OF THE LAKE:
My ears just can't believe it – why
become a human, destined to die?

RUSALKA:
Sám vyprávěls ty zvěsti neznámé,
že mají duši, jíž my nemáme,
a duše lidí že jde nebi vstříc,
když člověk zhyne a když znikne v nic!

VODNÍK:
Dokud rodná kolébá tě vlna,
nechtěj duši, ta je hříchu plna!

RUSALKA:
A plna lásky!

VODNÍK:
Vodo pravěká –
snad nemiluješ, dítě, člověka?

RUSALKA:
Sem často přichází
a v objetí mé stoupá,
šat shodí na hrázi
a v loktech mých se koupá.
Však pouhou vlnou jsem,
mou bytost nesmí zříti —
ó vím, že člověkem
dřív musila bych býti,
jak já jej objímám
a jak jej vinu v ruce,
by on mne objal sám
a zulíbal mne prudce!

RUSALKA:
Strange things you used to tell me of;
that they have souls which we do not,
and souls of humans go to heaven above,
that when they die their bodies turn to nought.

SPIRIT OF THE LAKE:
While cradled by your native wave,
a human soul full of sin do not crave!

RUSALKA:
But it's full of love!

SPIRIT OF THE LAKE:
The water world do not disgrace,
loving one of the human race!

RUSALKA:
He comes here often, yes,
and by the weir disrobes.
He enters my embrace;
held in my arms he bathes,
but I am just a wave, it's true,
a being hidden from his view.
I know that human form,
first of all, I must assume.
Then when once more he comes
and I wind him in my arms
he too will hold me close,
with hot passion in his kiss.

VODNÍK:
Dítě, dítě, z noci do noci
tvoje sestry budou pro tě plakat –
už ti není, není pomoci,
člověk-li tě v svou moc doveď zlákat!

RUSALKA:
Hastrmánku mužíčku,
on mne musí zočit –
pověz, pověz, tatíčku,
co mám smutná počít?

VODNÍK:
Ztracena, ztracena do věků,
prodána, prodána člověku!
Marno je lákat tě dolů v rej –
Ježibabu si zavolej,
ubohá rusalko bledá!...
 Potápí se.
Běda! Ó běda! Ó běda!
 Zmizí pod vodou.

RUSALKA:
Měsíčku na nebi hlubokém,
světlo tvé daleko vidí,
po světě bloudíš širokém,
díváš se v příbytky lidí.
Měsíčku, postůj chvíli,
řekni mi, kde je můj milý!

SPIRIT OF THE LAKE:
My child, each night your sisters one and all
will shed their tears for you,
for since a human has you in his thrall
there's nothing more that we can do.

RUSALKA:
He must behold me,
father dear, I know!
Tell me, tell me what to do,
I'm pining, pining so!

SPIRIT OF THE LAKE:
You're lost, you're lost for ever and a day,
to a human bartered away.
If paradise down here brings you sorrow,
you must call on Ježibaba,
poor pale Rusalka, go!
    He submerges.
Oh woe! Oh woe! Oh woe!
    He disappears below the surface of the lake.

RUSALKA:
Dear moon up in the deep dark sky,
your light can reach so very far.
You roam this world from up on high,
see people's homes, know where they are.
Please stay a while, dear moon, and say,
where is my love who's gone away?

Řekni mu, stříbrný měsíčku,
mé že jej objímá rámě,
aby si alespoň chviličku,
vzpomenul ve snění na mě.
Zasvěť mu do daleka,
řekni mu, kdo tu naň čeká!

O mně-li duše lidská sní,
ať se tou vzpomínkou vzbudí!
Měsíc zmizí v mracích.
Měsíčku, nehasni, nehasni!
Ta voda studí, ó, studí!

Zachvěje se úzkostí.
Ježibabo! Ježibabo!

VODNÍK – *pod vodou*:
Ubohá rusalko bledá!
Běda! Ó běda! Ó běda!

RUSALKA – *úpěnlivě*:
Ježibabo! Ježibabo!

JEŽIBABA – *v chalupě*:
Lkáním, štkáním, naříkáním
kdo mě budí před svítáním?

RUSALKA:
Ježibabo, léku dej mi,
vodní kouzlo se mne sejmi!

JEŽIBABA – *vychází z chalupy*:
Slyším cosi, čichám cosi –
ozvi se a pověz, kdo jsi!

O silver moon, give him a sign,
my arms it is that him entwine.
And may he dream he's with me once again,
for just a moment, now and then.
Light up his path and say
who here awaits him every day.

If his human soul dreams of me,
may he wake with this memory.
    The moon disappears behind the clouds.
Dear moon, don't fade away, oh don't fade!
The water is so cold, so cold!

    She trembles in trepidation.
Ježibaba! Ježibaba!

SPIRIT OF THE LAKE – *below the surface of the water*:
Poor pale Rusalka!
Oh woe! Oh woe! Oh woe!

RUSALKA – *pleading*:
Ježibaba! Ježibaba!

JEŽIBABA – *in her cottage*:
Such wailing, moaning, such heartache!
Who's waking me before daybreak?

RUSALKA:
O Ježibaba, work on me a spell,
the watery magic's hold dispel.

JEŽIBABA – *emerging from her cottage*:
What's that I hear, what's that I whiff?
Who's calling there? Speak up and tell.

RUSALKA:
Rusalka jsem, vodní víla,
dej mi léku, tetko milá!

JEŽIBABA – *se blíží k jezeru*:
Jsi-li víla, zjev se hbitě,
ukaž se mi, krásné dítě!

RUSALKA:
Vlnami jsem upoutána,
do leknínů zamotána.

JEŽIBABA:
Vytrhni se, cupy hupy
pospěš ke mně do chalupy—
pusť ji, vlnko, pusť ji ke mně,
ať se nožky dotknou země!
   Pomáhá rusalce na břeh.
Nožičky, držte ji, nožičky, neste ji—
vida, jak nožičky chodit už umějí!

RUSALKA – *jí klesne k nohám*:
Staletá moudrost tvá všechno ví,
proniklas přírody tajemství,
za nocí hlubokých o lidech sníš,
odvěkým živlům rozumíš,
pozemské jedy, paprsky měsíce
dovedeš svařit na léků tisíce,
dovedeš spojit, dovedeš bořit,
dovedeš usmrtit, dovedeš stvořit,
člověka v příšeru, příšeru v člověka
dovede proměnit moudrost tvá odvěká,
rusalky za nocí hrozbou svou strašíš,
pro lidské strasti divné léky snášíš,

RUSALKA:
Rusalka, I'm a water nymph.
Dear lady, cast on me a spell.

JEŽIBABA – *approaching the lake*:
If you're a nymph, appear at once.
Fair child, come here and show your face.

RUSALKA:
The waves hold me enchained,
in water lilies I'm entwined.

JEŽIBABA:
Then skip and hop and disentwine,
hurry along and dash to mine.
Wavelet, release this nymph I've found,
let her little feet tread the ground.
    She helps Rusalka onto the bank.
Come now, little legs – come now, come to me!
Those dainty feet soon learned to walk, you see!

RUSALKA – *kneeling before her*:
Your age-old wisdom knows it all,
Nature's secrets are at your beck and call.
You dream of folk at dead of night.
All the age-old forces you know aright.
From earthly poisons and from moonlight rays
with skill a thousand potions you devise.
Your skill can mend or devastate,
can put to death or yet create.
Your age-old wisdom is invoked, and then
men turn to monsters, monsters into men.
Your presence scares the water nymphs at night.
Strange cures you brew to set woes aright,

pro nás i pro lidi ve světě dalekém
sama jsi živlem, sama jsi člověkem,
se smrtí věčnost je tvé věno —
pomoz mi, pomoz mi, zázračná ženo!

JEŽIBABA:
To já znám, to já znám,
s takovou se chodí k nám!
Ale slyš, pilně slyš,
nežli léku okusíš:
perly máš, krásu máš –
pomohu-li, co mi dáš?

RUSALKA:
Vše, co mám, si vem –
ale udělej mě člověkem!

JEŽIBABA:
A nic víc? Pranic víc?
Proto přišlas úpějíc?
Voda tě už omrzela,
lidského jsi lačna těla,
milování, laškování,
hubiček a cukrování –
to já znám, to já znám,
s takovou se chodí k nám!

RUSALKA:
Tvoje moudrost všechno tuší –
dej mi lidské tělo, lidskou duši!

JEŽIBABA:
Dám ti, dám,
věz to rarach sám!

for us and folk the whole world through.
Eternal death awaits you too.
Primeval you are, yet you are human;
Help me, help me, wondrous woman.

JEŽIBABA:
Yes, I know, yes, I know –
the same old story once again!
But listen, nymph, before it's done –
you have pearls, you have beauty too.
Now, in return for this good turn,
what will I have from you?

RUSALKA:
Take all I have, it's yours.
Just make me human, please!

JEŽIBABA:
Is that all? No more?
That's what you're begging for?
The water's lost its old appeal.
Desire for human form is what you feel,
for loving and cuddling,
for kissing, billing and cooing.
Yes, I know – the same refrain,
the same old story once again!

RUSALKA:
You're wise, you've guessed it all –
give me a human body with its soul.

JEŽIBABA:
All right, I will,
by the devil!

Ale ty mi musíš dát
průsvitný svůj vodní šat,
a když lásky neokusíš na světě,
zavržena žíti musíš
v hlubinách zas prokletě.
Ztratíš-li tu lásku, po níž cit tvůj prahne,
kletba vodních mocí zas tě v hloubku stáhne,
a než nabudeš jí, trpět budeš též,
pro všechen sluch lidský něma zůstaneš!
Chceš být němá, chceš,
pro toho, jejž miluješ?

RUSALKA:
Jeho-li lásku poznat smím,
ráda, věř, pro něj oněmím!

JEŽIBABA:
Střez si ho, střez,
a věz to, věz:
prokleta-li se vrátíš ve vodníkovu říš,
miláčka svého také zahubíš,
stane se navždy obětí
věčného tvého prokletí!

RUSALKA:
Lidskou duší, čistou lidskou duší,
moje láska všechna kouzla zruší!

JEŽIBABA – *pomáhá rusalce*:
Tedy pojď, honem pojď,
do chaty mě doprovoď!
V krbu jedy uvaříme,
rusalku tím napojíme,
ale potom ani muk –
čury mury fuk!

(34)

For me you have to cast adrift
your diaphanous watery shift,
and if you fail to find love in the world,
back to the depths,
accursed, you will be hurled.
For if this love you crave you cannot keep,
my curse will draw you back into the deep.
Before you gain this love you'll suffer dear –
no word you say will humans hear.
For him you love,
you must be mute, is that clear?

RUSALKA:
If his love comes within my reach,
I'll gladly lose the gift of speech.

JEŽIBABA:
Take care of him
and be aware of this.
If you're accursed, you must again descend
into the deep. Your loved one will be damned.
He'll be the victim of your curse,
your eternal curse.

RUSALKA:
My human soul, my pure human soul,
and my true love, will banish every spell.

JEŽIBABA – *helping Rusalka*:
Then let's set off at once.
Come, hurry to my place!
We'll stir the poison in the cauldron.
Rusalka then shall drink the potion.
Henceforth she'll never speak a word.
Bubble, bubble, boiled and stirred!

Odvádí rusalku do chalupy, kdež zaplane červená záře.
Proud jisker vyrazí komínem, a z chalupy zazní čarování
ježibabino.

Lesní žínky, přilákány tím čarováním, se sbíhají
a nahlížejí do chalupy.

JEŽIBABA – *uvnitř*:
Čury mury fuk,
bílá pára vstává z luk!
Kapka krve dračí,
deset kapek žluče,
teplé srdce ptačí –
pokud ještě tluče.[2]
Skoč, můj mourku, skoč a skoč,
varem v kotli pozatoč!

Čury mury fuk,
nelekej se větších muk!
Toť tvé lidské věno,
a to musíš píti,
tím co uvařeno,
jazyk zdřevění ti.
Skoč můj mourku, holahej,
v hrdlo jí tu šťávu vlej!
Čury mury fuk,
ale teď už ani muk!

Ticho v chalupě.

Lesní žínky se rozprchly.

2) In an earlier edition: *už to z kotle hučí.*

She leads Rusalka to her cottage. A red glow flares
up inside. Sparks fly from the chimney and the witch's
incantation is heard.

The wood nymphs, attracted by the incantation,
run to the cottage and peer in at the window.

JEŽIBABA – *in her cottage*:
Bubble, bubble, stir it well!
White clouds of steam above the dell!
Blood of dragon, just a tad,
ten drops of bile,
warm heart of bird,
still beating meanwhile.
Jump to it, grimalkin,
stir the bubbles in the cauldron!

Stir it round, bubble, bubble,
Fear not, if there is trouble!
It's your human dowry,
and it must be swallowed.
This potion we have brewed
shall turn your tongue to wood.
Come, grimalkin, here we go,
Pour it down her, nice and slow!
Bubble, bubble, stirred around.
Now not another sound.

All is quiet in the cottage.

The wood nymphs scatter.

Obloha se jasní,
z daleka znějí lovecké rohy.

VODNÍK – *hluboko pod vodou:*
Ubohá rusalko bledá!
Běda! Ó běda! Ó běda!

Nad jezerem se rdí jitřní záře.

LOVEC – *zpívá v daleku:*
Jel mladý lovec, jel a jel,
laň bílou v lese uviděl,
hluboké oči laň měla.
– Zdali ji stihne má střela?

Ó, mladý lovče, dále spěj,
tu bílou laňku nestřílej,
varuj se jejího těla!
– Zdali ji stihne má střela?

PRINC – *vyrazí z lesa s kuší v ruce:*
Zde mihla se a zase zmizela!
Horem a dolem, lesem a polem
podivná zvěř ta míhá se kolem –
a tady stopa znikla docela!
A tajemným vlněním potají
ty vody mě v lokty své lákají,
jak bych měl divoký lovu cit
v objetí jejich zas ochladit.
Krok vázne mi, stesk cítím neznámý,
zbraň z unavené ruky padá mi,
sotva lov začal, unavil mne vráz,
divné to kouzlo zajalo mě zas!

*The sky clears and the sound of hunting horns
is heard in the distance.*

SPIRIT OF THE LAKE – *deep below the surface of the lake:*
Poor pale Rusalka!
Oh woe! Oh woe! Oh woe!

A red dawn sky is seen over the lake.

HUNTSMAN – *singing in the distance*:
A youthful huntsman on a forest ride
a pure white doe at length espied.
She gazed intently, wide-eyed doe.
Will I claim her with my bow?

Young huntsman, go, move on.
Don't shoot this doe, no not this one.
Beware of her, she's charmed, you know!
Will I claim her with my bow?

PRINCE – *dashes out of the forest, holding a crossbow*:
She flashes by and then she's gone,
through woods, through fields, up hill, down dale,
strange creature flitting by, then on and on.
Upon this spot we've lost her trail.
These waters ripple, working charms,
they lure me in with open arms,
as if the wild ardour of the chase
should be abated in their embrace.
I feel longings unknown, slow is my gait,
my weary arms allow my bow to fall,
only just begun, the chase tires me out.
This spell's so strange; it has me in its thrall.

LOVEC – *nablízku*:
Laň nebyla to – lovče, stůj!
Bůh tvoji duši opatruj!
Srdce tvé smutno je zcela...
Koho to stihla tvá střela?

Lovci vyjdou z lesa.

PRINC:
Ustaňte v lovu, na hrad vraťte se,
podivné čáry bloudí po lese,
divnější čáry v duši mám –
vraťte se domů, chci býti sám!

Lovci odcházejí.
Princ usedne zadumán na břehu jezera.

Rusalka vyšla z chalupy. Je bosa, v popelavých šatech
nuzného dítěte. Krásné její zlaté vlasy hluboko splývají.
Je němá.

PRINC – *spatřiv ji vyskočí*:
Vidino divná, přesladká,
jsi-li ty člověk nebo pohádka?
Přišla jsi chránit vzácné zvěři,
kterou jsem zahléd' v lesa šeři?
Přišla-lis prosit za ni,
sestřičko bílých laní?
Anebo sama, jak vstříc mi jdeš,
kořistí lovcovou býti chceš?

Rusalka vztáhne k němu němě své ruce.

HUNTSMAN – *approaching*:
That was no doe. Wait, huntsman, stay!
May God preserve you safe and sound.
Your heart's distraught for sure today.
Who can it be your arrow's found?

   Huntsmen emerge from the forest.

PRINCE:
Call off the chase now! Ride back home!
Here in the woods strange spells abound.
Yet stranger spells besiege my mind.
Now go, ride back. Leave me alone.

   The huntsmen depart.
   The prince sits on the shore of the lake.

   Rusalka emerges from the cottage, barefoot, dressed
   as a destitute child. She has beautiful, long golden hair.
   She is mute.

PRINCE – *leaps to his feet on seeing her.*
O wondrous vision, lovely, pale,
are you a human or a fairy tale,
come to that rarest creature's aid
I glimpsed just now within the forest glade?
Come you to intercede,
for sister does to plead?
Or would you, approaching me this way,
become the huntsman's game I bag today?

   Rusalka silently stretches out her arms towards him.

PRINC:
Svírá ti ústa tajemství,
či navždy jazyk tvůj ztich'?
Něma-li ústa tvá, Bůh to ví,
vylíbám odpověď s nich!
Odpověď záhadám, jež mě sem zlákaly,
jež mě sem volaly přes trní, přes skály,
abych tu konečně v blažený dnešní den,
dítě, tvým pohledem náhle byl okouzlen!
Co v srdci tvém je ukryto,
máš-li mě ráda, zjev mi to!

Rusalka mu padne do náručí.

RUSALKY – *pod vodou*:
Sestry, jedna schází z nás!

Rusalka polekána se vzchopí a naslouchá.

RUSALKY:
Sestřičko, kam odešlas?

Rusalka se chvěje nerozhodností a bázní.

VODNÍK – *pod vodou*:
Přes hory, doly a lesy!

RUSALKY:
Sestřičko, sestřičko, kde jsi?

Rusalka se stulí úzkostně v náručí princově.

PRINCE:
Are your lips sealed by some strange will?
Must your tongue be forever still?
Well if your lips can't speak of this,
by God, I'll make them answer with a kiss.
They'll tell me of the mystery that's drawn
me, called me over rock and thorn
this wondrous day, enchanting me at once,
my child, as suddenly I see your face.
What does your heart conceal?
If you love me, show me what you feel.

Rusalka falls into his arms.

WATER NYMPHS – *below the surface of the lake*:
Sisters, one of us has gone!

Rusalka gives a start and listens in alarm.

WATER NYMPHS:
O sister dear, where are you, missing one?

Rusalka trembles in indecision and fear.

SPIRIT OF THE LAKE – *below the surface of the lake:*
Up hill, down dale and on and on.

WATER NYMPHS:
Sister, dear sister, where have you gone?

Rusalka huddles in trepidation in the prince's embrace.

PRINC:
Vím, žes jen kouzlo, které mine
a rozplyne se v mlžný rej,
však dokud čas náš neuplyne,
ó pohádko má, neprchej!
Můj skončen lov – nač myslit naň?
Tys nejvzácnější moje laň,
hvězdička zlatá v noc temnou –
pohádko moje, pojď se mnou!

Odvádí rusalku.

PRINCE:
I know you're magic that cannot last,
bound to vanish in a whirl of mist,
but till our time is up please stay,
my fairy tale, do not run away!
The chase is over, time to go.
You are my dear, most precious doe,
bright star, in the dark night you shine –
my fairy tale, come, be mine!

He leads Rusalka away.

*Sad na zámku princově. V pozadí sloupořadí a slavnostní
síň hodovní. V popředí pod starými stromy zátoka jezerní.
Je kvečeru.*

ACT TWO

An orchard in the grounds of the prince's castle.
In the background a colonnade and a banqueting hall.
In the foreground an inlet of the lake beneath mature trees.
It is late afternoon.

HAJNÝ – *přichází s kuchtíkem*:
Jářku, jařku, klouče milé,
honem tedy dopověz,
jakáže to kratochvíle
na zámku se strojí dnes?
To je hostí na síni,
to je práce v kuchyni,
na stolech a na policích
podivného náčiní!

KUCHTÍK:
Máme ti teď sháňku,
milý strýče Vaňku,
do večera od svítání
neustanem v práci ani!
Princ ti našel v lese
divné stvoření,
a s ním, podivme se,
snad se ožení!
Našel prý ji v lesích tvých,
ve tvých lesích hlubokých –
ale ať ji vzal kde vzal,
já bych se jí, strýčku, bál!
Holka je ti němá,
kapky krve nemá,
chodí jako vyjevená –
To by byla čistá žena!

HAJNÝ:
Je to pravda vskutku,
co se mluví všude?
Můj ty milý smutku,
už to takhle bude!
Ať nás Pánbůh chrání,
myslivec jsem starý –

GAMEKEEPER – *approaching with the kitchen hand:*
Well now, my lad, what's this you say?
Let's hear the rest. I know there's more.
What entertainment is in store
here in the castle grounds today?
So many guests already there,
the kitchen busy as can be,
and strange utensils everywhere
on tables and shelves I see.

KITCHEN HAND:
We're fair rushed off our feet,
it's all go and we're dead beat.
We have to work from morn till night,
without a moment of respite.
Out in the woods the prince has found
some creature – well, she is right weird.
And though it's quite beyond belief,
they say she'll soon become his wife!
I'm told he found her in a glade,
within your forest deep and dark.
But be that true, or idle talk,
of her I'd be afraid!
The girl's struck dumb, you see;
no single drop of blood has she.
She looks bewildered, seems to me;
fine wife indeed I'm sure she'd be!

GAMEKEEPER:
O can this really be,
is what they say all true?
O goodness gracious me,
look what it's coming to!
May God keep us from harm,
my woodsman's nouse can tell

že v tom milování
vězí divné čáry!
U nás v lese straší
šlakovité moci,
lesem divní braši
chodí o půlnoci.
Je-li v těle duše slabá,
uhrane ji Ježibaba,
pode hrází tuze snadno
hastrman tě stáhne na dno.
A kdo vidí lesní žínky
bez košilky, bez sukýnky,
omámí ho lásky chtíč –
Pánbůh s námi a zlý pryč!

KUCHTÍK:
Já se bojím, strýčku!

HAJNÝ:
Inu, není div –
buď ti, pacholíčku,
Pánbůh milostiv!

KUCHTÍK:
Náš princ vždy tak švarný byl –
kterak se teď proměnil!
Není, jaký býval, není,
bloudí jako omámen,
stará Háta na modlení
dává za něj den co den.
A pan farář, jak to slyšel,
varovat ti prince přišel –
ale princ ne a ne,
holka prý tu zůstane!

this love match is a charm;
it's worked by some strange spell.
Dread powers haunt us here,
strange creatures are about;
at midnight they come out,
arouse in us dread fear.
Ježibaba can always tell
the faint at heart – they draw her spell.
Approach a weir – before you know,
Water Spirit drags you below.
A man who sees wood nymphs at play –
their flimsy shifts all cast away –
succumbs to lust, they so enthral.
Such ills! – may God preserve us all!

KITCHEN HAND:
Oh, uncle, I'm so scared!

GAMEKEEPER:
Oh well, no wonder!
With God's grace you'll be spared,
poor little sinner!

KITCHEN HAND:
He always was our dashing prince
but now he's very changed, alas!
Unlike the man he used to be,
he just wanders in reverie.
Old Hattie's worried too –
she prays for him each day.
The priest, when told of this to-do,
came round to warn him straight away.
To that the prince just said "nay, nay!"
He said the wench would stay.

HAJNÝ:
Proto jsou tu hosté již,
proto se tak prázdní špíž!
Proto jsem honem vlek'
plno zvěře na zámek!

KUCHTÍK:
Na štěstí, jak zdá se,
nemělo to být,
všechno může zase
jiná pokazit!
Stará Háta vypráví,
princ že prý je vrtkavý;
už prý jeho láska mizí,
jinou prý zas v mysli má,
po jakési kněžně cizí,
hází prý už očima!

HAJNÝ:
Pánbůh dej, Pánbůh dej,
ve zdraví ho zachovej!
Já být princem, bez okolků
vyhnal bych tu cizí holku,
než mě v čáry zamotá –
ať se klidí, žebrota!

KUCHTÍK – *náhle*:
Hu, tam si vede princ tu obludu!
    Uteče.

HAJNÝ:
Já na ní taky čekat nebudu!
    Uteče jinudy.

GAMEKEEPER:
That's why these guests are all here,
that's why the larder's so bare.
That's why I have, real quick,
to lug much game for you to cook.

KITCHEN HAND:
With any luck, it seems,
it never was to be;
someone else, maybe,
will ruin all her dreams.
Old Hattie's just been telling me
how fickle our prince can be.
His love's already all but dead;
another's got into his head –
some foreign princess, she says –
for her alone he now has eyes.

GAMEKEEPER:
The Lord be praised, the Lord be praised!
May God preserve him safe and sound!
If I was the prince, truth to tell,
I'd chase that weird wench away
before she dragged me down to Hell.
The beggar girl should go today!

KITCHEN HAND – *abruptly*:
Here comes the prince, that weird creature too.
   He runs off.

GAMEKEEPER:
Well, I won't stay! I'm off without ado.
   He runs off in a different direction.

PRINC – *přichází za chvíli poté s rusalkou*
krásně oděnou:
Již týden dlíš mi po boku,
jak z báje zjev dlíš přede mnou,
a marně v očí hluboku
tvou bytost hledám tajemnou.
Má sňatek dát mi teprve,
co láska dávno chtěla,
bys rozhořela do krve
a byla ženou zcela?
Proč chladí tvoje objetí,
vzplát vášní proč se zdráhá?
Proč úzkostí jen zachvěti
se mám v tvých loktech drahá?
Však marně, marně dusím smutný cit,
z tvé náruče se nelze vyprostit –
bys byla stokrát chladná, nesmělá,
mít musím tebe, musím docela!

CIZÍ KNĚŽNA – *přichází pozadím; spatříc prince*
a rusalku:
Ne, není to láska – jen hněvný je to cit,
že jiná dlí, kde já jsem chtěla být,
a že jsem jeho býti neměla,
ať štěstí obou zhyne docela!
   Pokročí.
Princ na chvíli zda vzpomene si přec,
že hostitelem jest i milenec?
Má na to štěstí, jímž vás blaží svět,
i cizí host váš němě pohlížet?
   Stane mezi princem a rusalkou.

PRINCE – *approaching shortly afterwards with Rusalka,*
who is exquisitely dressed.
A week you've bided by my side,
the fairy tale vision that I met.
In vain I gaze in your eyes open wide;
your secret being eludes me yet.
Will love's desire be won at last
only once the wedding feast has passed,
and unbridled passion springs to life
as then you really do become my wife?
O why is your embrace so cold,
all your passion still withheld?
Why must I tremble with fear,
held in your arms, my dear?
In vain, in vain I stifle my sadness,
I can't escape from your embrace.
Cold and timid though you are, so aloof,
I must make you mine, all mine, my love!

FOREIGN PRINCESS – *approaching on seeing the prince*
with Rusalka:
No it's not love, I'm angry, seeing red;
another's taken over in my stead.
And since I could not be his as I wished,
may their happiness be for ever dashed!
    She steps forward.
Has it slipped the lover's mind, I wonder,
what obligations he as host is under?
Should I, a foreign guest, look on,
mutely observe the joys you've won?
    She steps between the prince and Rusalka.

PRINC – *se vzruší, sotvaže spatřil kněžnu*:
Ach, výčitka to věru včasná,
a s vašich rtíků rád ji snáším –
i ženich věru, kněžno krásná,
je především jen sluhou vaším!

CIZÍ KNĚŽNA – *pohlédnouc na rusalku*:
A vaše kráska, citů vašich paní,
vás nepokárá za to slůvkem ani?
  Jízlivě:
Či v pohledu svém tolik něhy má,
že mluví s vámi pouze očima?

PRINC – *v rozpacích*:
Však oči její říci zapomněly,
že hostitel se nepozorným stal –
nechť nahradí teď rychle, svolíte-li,
co roztržit jen chvíli zanedbal!
  Podává kněžně ruku.

  Rusalka se chytne křečovitě ruky princovy.

PRINC:
Nač rozpaky tvoje? A proč se tolik chvíš?
V svou komnatu pospěš a stroj se k plesu již!
  Odvádí kněžnu.

CIZÍ KNĚŽNA – *odcházejíc rusalce*:
Ó, vystrojte se v šaty přebohaté –
mám jeho dvornost, vy však lásku máte!
  Odejde s princem.

*Rusalka ztrnule hledí za nimi, jako by pohledem
chtěla prince zadržet, ale pak smutna a zlomena odchází
sloupořadím.*

PRINCE – *aroused at the sight of the foreign princess*:
Ah, this timely reproach indeed,
from your soft lips I'll gladly heed.
Even the bridegroom, beautiful princess,
is your servant above all else.

FOREIGN PRINCESS – *glancing at Rusalka*:
But your love, mistress of your heart,
won't she chastise you with words that hurt?
    Sarcastically:
Or does she give you such a tender look
that you can always read her like a book?

PRINCE – *embarrassed*:
But her eyes forgot to say
the host's attention's drawn away.
For his neglect, if you allow,
he'll make amends right now.
    He offers the princess his arm.

    Rusalka nervously seizes the prince's hand.

PRINCE:
What troubles you? Why do you tremble so?
Dress quickly for the ball, it's time to go.
    He leads the princess away.

FOREIGN PRINCESS – *to Rusalka, as she departs*:
O! Wear your most luxurious dress, please do!
He's courting me – his heart belongs to you.
    She leaves with the prince.

*Rusalka watches helplessly, as though she wants to deter
the prince, but then, sad and defeated, she departs along
the colonnade.*

Zatím se sšeřilo, večer hasne, a později zasvítne měsíc.
V síních zazní slavnostní hudba a zaplanou světla.
Je vidět slavnostní ruch, hosté se scházejí a tvoří skupiny.
Později zpěv a tanec.

VODNÍK – *se zatím vynořil ze zátoky*:
Ubohá rusalko bledá,
v nádheru světa zakletá!
Celý svět nedá ti, nedá,
vodní čím říše rozkvétá!
Stokrát bys byla člověkem,
ve jhu jsi spjata odvěkém,
byť měl tě člověk stokrát rád,
navždy ho nemůžeš upoutat!

Ubohá rusalko bledá,
zajatá v kouzlo lidských pout!
Voda tvá všude tě hledá,
nadarmo chce tě obejmout!
Až se zas vrátíš k družkám svým,
budeš jen živlem smrtícím,
vrátíš se žitím uvadlá,
prokletí živlů jsi propadla!

ZPĚV – *v síni*:
Květiny bílé po cestě,
po cestě všude kvetly,
hoch jel a jel k své nevěstě,
a den se smál tak světlý.

Nemeškej, hochu, k milé spěš,
dorosteš záhy v muže,
zpátky až tudy pojedeš,
pokvetou rudé růže.

Meanwhile, dusk has fallen, then darkness follows. Later,
the moon comes out. In the hall, ceremonial music strikes
up and lights come on. Amongst the proceedings, groups
of guests are seen. Later, singing and dancing begin.

SPIRIT OF THE LAKE – *surfacing meanwhile in the inlet*:
My poor Rusalka, so, so pale;
the wondrous world has you in thrall!
You'll never find in all the world
water realm's delights, they're denied.
You could be human a hundredfold,
yet still be fettered by our bonds of old.
Though a human may love you to despair
you cannot make him yours for ever.

My poor Rusalka, so, so pale;
those human charms have you in thrall!
Your watery home seeks you in vain;
they'd fain embrace you once again,
but on return to your own kind
you'd bring but death, they'd find.
By life you're altered for the worse;
you've succumbed to an elemental curse.

CHORUS – *in the hall*:
White flowers on our way,
were blooming all the way.
To meet his bride the youth rode on apace;
the day wore a bright smiling face.

To your love, lad, hurry along,
grown man you'll be ere long;
when you return this way again
red roses will be blooming then.

Květiny bílé nejdříve
úpalem slunce zašly,
ale ty růže ohnivé
svatební lože krášlí!

*Princ se objeví chvílemi v slavnostním ruchu
a dvoří se okázale cizí kněžně.*

VODNÍK:
Na vodách bílý leknín sní,
smutným ti druhem bude,
pro tvoje lože svatební
nekvetou růže rudé!

*Rusalka vyběhne zoufalá ze síně
a prchá sadem.*

VODNÍK – *překvapen*:
Rusalko, dcerko, znáš mne, znáš?

RUSALKA – *náhle nabyvši řeči vykřikne*:
Vodníku, tatíčku drahý!

VODNÍK:
Proto jsem přišel v zámek váš,
bych zřel tě truchlit tak záhy?

RUSALKA:
Tatíčku vodníku, spas mě, spas,
úzkost mě pojala hrozná!
Běda, že chtěla jsem zradit vás,
běda, kdo člověka pozná!

White flowers faded soon,
shrivelled in the blazing sun,
but roses flaming red
adorn the bridal bed!

*The prince appears from time to time amongst
the ceremonial proceedings, ostentatiously courting
the foreign princess.*

SPIRIT OF THE LAKE:
White water lilies dreaming on the lake,
what sad companions they will make;
for your marriage bed,
no blooming roses red!

*Rusalka runs out from the hall in deep despair,
running across the orchard.*

SPIRIT OF THE LAKE – *taken aback*:
Daughter dear, look who's here!

RUSALKA – *suddenly acquiring speech, she calls out:*
Spirit of the Lake, father dear!

SPIRIT OF THE LAKE:
To your castle I wend my way,
so soon must I behold your dismay?

RUSALKA:
Oh save me, save me, father dear,
I'm gripped by anguish, full of fear.
Alas – I betrayed you, I know;
to love a human spells such woe.

Jiná jej krásou jala vráz,
divokou lidskou krásou –
a mne už nezná, nezná zas
rusalku prostovlasou!

VODNÍK:
On že tě zavrh', jenž měl tě rád?
Musíš teď, musíš vytrvat!

RUSALKA:
Ó marno, marno, marno to je,
a prázdnota je v srdci mém,
jsou marny všechny vděky moje,
když zpola jen jsem člověkem!
Jí hoří v očích vášně síla,
té lidské vášně prokleté,
mě chladná voda porodila,
a nemám, nemám vášně té!
Prokleta vámi, pro něj ztracena,
odvěkých živlů lichá ozvěna
ženou ni vílou nemohu být,
nemohu zemřít, nemohu žít!

Princ přichází sadem s cizí kněžnou.

RUSALKA – *přitulí se k vodníkovi*:
Vidíš je, vidíš? Jsou tu zas –
tatíčku, tatíčku, spas mě, spas!

CIZÍ KNĚŽNA:
Vám v očích divný žár se zračí
a naslouchám vám zmámena,
jste stále vřelejší a sladší –
ó princi, co to znamená?

Another fills him with desire,
a human beauty, wild as fire –
he forgets me, knows me no more,
a water nymph modest and pure.

SPIRIT OF THE LAKE:
Does he who loved you spurn you now?
You must persist somehow.

RUSALKA:
O, it's in vain, it's all in vain,
there's emptiness within my heart,
the charms I have are all in vain
since I'm not human – only part!
The flame of passion's in her eyes,
that cursed passion humans prize!
I was born of water, cool and fresh;
such passion I cannot unleash!
Cursed by you all, and lost to him,
the deaf echo of an ancient force,
neither nymph nor woman am I.
I cannot live! I cannot die!

The prince enters the orchard with the foreign princess.

RUSALKA – *snuggling up to Spirit of the Lake*:
See them, see them? Again they're here!
Save me, save me, father dear!

FOREIGN PRINCESS:
The strangest glow is in your eyes;
I hear your words as in a daze.
Your passion and charm know no bounds.
O prince, say what this portends.

Kam prchla vaše vyvolená,
ta bez řeči a beze jména,
kam prchla, aby viděla,
že princ je změněn docela?

PRINC:
Kam prchla? Milý Bůh to ví!
Však změnou tou jste sama vinna,
a letní noc to nepoví,
že zajala mě kouzla jiná.
Ó, nazvete to rozmarem,
že miloval jsem jinou chvíli,
a buďte žhavým požárem,
kde dosud luny svit plál bílý!

CIZÍ KNĚŽNA:
Až požár můj vás popálí,
a všechny vaše vášně zděsí,
až odejdu vám do dáli,
co s leskem luny počnete si?
Až obejmou vás lokty sličné
té němé krásky náměsíčné,
čím k vášni hřát se budete?
Ó, škoda, škoda vášně té!
Ó teprve teď poznávám,
že námluvy mi náhle kynou –
pan ženich, zdá se, neví sám,
zda namlouvá si mě, či jinou!

PRINC – *rozvášněn*:
A kdyby celý svět
chtěl klnout mojí touze,
jste vy ten rudý květ,
byť kvetl chvíli pouze!

Where has your bride now fled away,
who has no speech, nor name, they say?
Where has she fled, and can she see
the prince has changed entirely?

PRINCE:
Dear God alone knows where she's fled.
This change is all your fault, it must be said,
but the summer night will never tell
I'm captivated by another spell.
Yes, once in my capricious ways
I loved another for a while,
but you will be a fiery blaze
where luna's rays till now shone pale.

FOREIGN PRINCESS:
Once you're burned by my wildfire,
and driven wild with passion,
when far from you I then retire,
will moonbeams give you satisfaction?
When that mute beauty's fair arms hold you tight,
embrace you in the pale moonlight,
how then will your ardour be aroused?
It's such a shame the flame is doused.
O, now at last I see
quite suddenly he's courting me;
it seems the bridegroom can't decide
which one of us should be his bride.

PRINCE – *becoming passionate*:
I care not that the world may blame
my protestations of desire;
you are my flower all aflame,
however soon be quenched your fire.

Ó, teprve teď vím,
čím mřelo moje tělo,
když lásky tajemstvím
se uzdraviti chtělo!
Co zbude z oné lásky,
jíž v osidla jsem pad'?
Rád strhám všecky svazky,
bych vás moh' milovat!
Vášnivě obejme cizí kněžnu.

Rusalka se vytrhne z objetí vodníkova
a vrhá se k princi.

PRINC – *poděšen*:
Mrazí mě tvoje ramena,
bílá ty kráso studená!
Odstrčí rusalku.

VODNÍK – *se zjeví v plném světle měsíčním;*
příšerným hlasem:
V jinou spěš náruč, spěš a spěš –
tomuto objetí neujdeš!
Strhne rusalku do jezera.

PRINC – *ohromen*:
Z objetí moci tajemné,
spaste mne, spaste mne, spaste mne!
Vrhá se cizí kněžně k nohám.

CIZÍ KNĚŽNA – *s divým smíchem*:
V hlubinu pekla rozevřenou,
pospěšte za svou vyvolenou!
Odchází.

Only now I know
what ailed my body so,
when it sought your succour –
love's secret endeavour.
What of that love remains
that trapped me in a snare?
I'd gladly loose those chains;
love you I would dare.
He passionately embraces the foreign princess.

*Rusalka tears herself from Spirit of the Lake's
embrace and rushes towards the prince.*

PRINCE – *in alarm*:
I freeze in your embrace,
pale beauty, cold as ice.
He pushes Rusalka away.

SPIRIT OF THE LAKE – *appears in the full light of the moon.
In a terrifying tone of voice*:
Go to another's arms; do not delay –
from this embrace you'll never get away!
He pulls Rusalka into the lake.

PRINCE – *astounded*:
A magic power clutches me,
save me, save me, save me!
He falls to his knees before the foreign princess.

FOREIGN PRINCESS – *laughing wildly*:
Into the maw of Hell, gaping wide,
go, hasten to your chosen bride!
She departs.

Palouk na pokraji jezera jako prve. Chýlí se k večeru,
obloha je pod mrakem.

ACT THREE

A glade on the shore of a lake, as at the beginning.
Late afternoon. The sky is overcast.

RUSALKA – *sedí na břehu jezera, bílá a bledá;*
vlasy jí zpopelavěly, oči pohasly:
Necitelná vodní moci,
kážeš mi zas v hlubinu –
proč v tvém chladu bez pomoci
nezhynu, ach, nezhynu?
Mladosti své pozbavena,
bez radosti sester svých,
pro svou lásku odsouzena
zmizím v proudech studených.
Ztrativši svůj půvab sladký,
miláčkem svým prokleta,
marně toužím k sestrám zpátky,
marně toužím do světa.
Kde jste, kouzla letních nocí
nad kalichy leknínů?
Proč v tom chladu bez pomoci
nezhynu, ach, nezhynu?

JEŽIBABA – *přichází z lesa:*
I vida, už ses navrátila?
No tos tam dlouho nepobyla!
A jak máš smutné tvářičky,
a jak tu truchlíš o samotě!
Což, nechutnaly hubičky
a lidské lože nehřálo tě?

RUSALKA:
Ach běda, běda, tetko rozmilá,
vše zradilo mě, vše jsem ztratila!

JEŽIBABA:
Krátké bylo milování,
dlouhé bude naříkání,

RUSALKA – *sits on the shore of the lake, white and pale;
her hair has turned an ashen grey and the sparkle has gone
from her eyes:*
Heartless watery power,
you cast me in the deep for ever.
I'm helpless, cold as cold, but why
can I not die, oh why can I not die?
My youth's been taken away,
no sisters left with whom to play.
For love condemned, I go
to chilly waters down below.
I've lost my former charms and graces;
accursed by my dearest one,
in vain I long to see my sisters' faces,
all hopes of being human — gone.
Where are you, charms of summer nights,
with those water-lily cups, my delights?
I'm helpless, cold as cold; oh why
can I not die, can I not die?

JEŽIBABA – *emerging from the forest*:
You're back again so soon, my dear?
Your stay was brief, I fear!
How sad your little face.
So lonely bitter tears you shed!
Not so sweet, the human's kiss?
Not nice and warm, the human's bed?

RUSALKA:
Oh, woe, dear lady, my downfall!
By all betrayed, I've lost it all!

JEŽIBABA:
This love you could not long sustain,
but very long you will complain.

po hubičkách mužských úst
nekonečný, věčný půst!
Člověk je člověk, živlů vyvrhel,
z kořenů země dávno vyvrácen –
běda, kdo jeho lásku poznat chtěl,
jeho kdo zradou je teď zatracen!

RUSALKA:
Tetko má moudrá, tetko, rci,
není mi, není pomoci?

JEŽIBABA:
Miláček tě zavrh', přestal tě mít rád –
a teď Ježibaba má zas pomáhat?
Po záletech světských, dcerko rozmilá,
bys teď k sestrám ráda se zas vrátila?
Inu, mám já radu, dobrou radu mám,
ale poslechneš-li, ví to rarach sám!
Lidskou krví musíš smýti
živlů prokletí
za lásku, již chtělas míti
v lidském objetí.
Budeš zas, čím bylas prve,
než tě zklamal svět –
ale horkem lidské krve
lze jen ozdravět.
Opustí tě všechna muka,
šťastna budeš hned,
zahubí-li tvoje ruka
toho, jenž tě sved'!

RUSALKA – zděšena:
Ó, Ježibabo, běda, co to chceš?

Sweet were the kisses from the lips of man,
but now you face an endless ban.
A human is but human, nature's slime,
uprooted from the earth since ancient time.
Woe on her who for his love did thirst,
for now she is betrayed by him, she's cursed.

RUSALKA:
Tell me dear lady, for you're so wise,
help me, help; what do you advise?

JEŽIBABA:
Your lover's left you – his love did not last –
now Ježibaba must help, as in the past?
You've seen the world, my child, and once again
you'd like to join your sisters' own domain.
This good advice I now propose,
but will you take it? – Devil only knows!
With human blood you must erase
the curse of elemental laws,
– you loved a human, that's the cause –
you longed for his embrace.
You'll be again the carefree wraith
you were before the world betrayed your faith.
Hot human blood can yet restore
your former health once more.
At once your woes will fade away,
your happiness return the day
that your seducer dies –
at your own hand meets his demise.

RUSALKA – *horrified*:
Ježibaba, what did you say?

JEŽIBABA – *vytáhne ze záňadří nůž*
a vtiskne jej rusalce:
Ten vezmi nůž a slib, že poslechneš!

RUSALKA – *zahodí nůž do jezera*:
Jde z tebe hrůza; nech mne, nech!
Chci věčně trpět v úzkostech,
chci věčně cítit kletbu svou,
svou celou lásku zhrzenou,
svou beznaděj chci všechnu zřít –
však on, on musí spasen být!

JEŽIBABA – *se rozchechtá:*
V lidský život potměšilý
touha tvá tě vábila – ·
a teď nemáš tolik síly,
lidskou krev bys prolila?
Člověk je člověkem teprve,
v cizí krev ruku když ztopil,
vášní když zbrocen až do krve
bližního krví se opil.
A ty žes chtěla člověkem být,
člověka vášní omámit?
Prázdná ty vodní bublinečko,
měsíčná bledá zahalečko,
jdi, trp a trp si z věků do věků
a zeschni touhou po svém člověku!
    Odbelhá se do chalupy.

RUSALKA:
Vyrvanou životu
v hlubokou samotu,
volá mě, volá říše má;
miláčku, vím to, vím,

JEŽIBABA – *draws a knife from her bosom
and presses it into Rusalka's hand*:
Just take this knife and promise you'll obey!

RUSALKA – *casting the knife into the lake*:
You horrify me, let me be!
I'd rather face eternal agony.
I will for ever bear this dreadful curse
and unrequited love, what could be worse? –
submitting to my fate, my own hopes waived,
for he must, he must be saved!

JEŽIBABA – *bursts into laughter*:
Lured by passions that you seek
into the human world's falsehood,
suddenly you are too weak
to spill a human's blood?
A human is a human only when
by his hand another's blood is shed,
when passion's aroused and he is then
intoxicated by a brother's blood.
You say you wanted to be human
and captivate a man with passion,
You wan water spray, you empty bubble,
ephemeral, pale moonlight ray!
Go, suffer then, for evermore you must;
yearning for your man, you'll turn to dust.
    She hobbles off to her cottage.

RUSALKA:
Outcast am I from life,
a solitary waif.
My realm now calls, it calls, and so,
my dearest love, I know,

budu tvým prokletím –
běda nám, běda oběma!
  Ponoří se do jezera.

RUSALKY – *pod vodou:*
Odešla jsi do světa,
uprchla jsi našim hrám,
sestřičko ty prokletá,
nesestupuj k nám!

V naše tance nesmí sem,
koho člověk objal již –
rozprchnem se, rozprchnem,
jak se přiblížíš!

Z tvého smutku vane strach
v radostný náš hravý rej –
s bludičkami v bažinách
za nocí si hrej!

Lákej lidi svitem svým,
na rozcestích těkej teď,
světýlkem svým modravým
do hrobu jim svěť!

Na hrobech a rozcestích
jiných sester najdeš rej,
v reje vodních sester svých
už se nevracej!

  Ticho. Na západě rudnou červánky.

I'm your damnation, I'm your curse.
We both are damned – woe is us!
　　She submerges in the lake.

WATER NYMPHS – *below the surface of the lake*:
Into the world you went away,
you fled the games we play.
O sister, you are damned, my dear,
do not return to us down here!

None who's known a man's embrace
may join us in our dance.
We'll flee, away we'll fly
if ever you come by.

Your sadness gives us fright,
disturbs our fun and games.
Will o' the wisp, you'll fly by night
above the swamp, your new domain.

Your light will lure the folk below
at crossroads as you flit and rave;
your faintly bluish glow
will light them to their graves!

By crossroads and by graves you'll find
new sisters' games to play.
Where sisters of the water frolic, mind,
you must stay away.

　　Silence. Red rays of sunset light up the western sky.

HAJNÝ – *přivádí kuchtíka*:
Že se bojíš? Třesky plesky,
však tu jiní bývávali!
Zaklepej a pověz hezky,
co ti doma přikázali:
princ že nosí těžkou dumu,
že se poplet' na rozumu,
jakás pekla stvůra klatá,
že k vám přišla do hradu,
a že prosí stará Háta
Ježibabu o radu!

KUCHTÍK – *se vzpouzí*:
Mně už chromne noha,
vlčí mlhu mám –
pro živého Boha,
strýčku, jdi tam sám!

HAJNÝ:
Kolikrát jsem tudy šel,
temno leckdy bývalo již –
tys mi čistý strašpytel,
že se staré babky bojíš!

KUCHTÍK:
Ondy, když jsi u nás byl,
sáms mě, strýčku, postrašil,
nediv se teď, milý brachu,
že mám v lese plno strachu!

HAJNÝ:
Řeči sem, řeči tam,
to tak někdy přidávám!
Ale teď honem hleď

GAMEKEEPER – *bringing with him the kitchen hand*:
You're scared? Oh piffle! Nought to fear.
You're not the first to visit here.
Now knock and tell her why you've come,
just as they told you back at home.
The prince has something on his mind.
He's quite distraught, we find.
Some cursed creature out of Hell
came to our castle, cast a spell.
Old Hattie asks the witch's view;
Ježibaba, tell us what to do!

KITCHEN HAND – *resisting him*:
My legs begin to shake,
my eyes are blurred, I cannot see,
Oh uncle, for goodness sake,
go on without me!

GAMEKEEPER:
Many a time I've passed this way,
it often was at dead of night,
so you're a scaredypants then, eh?
Does this old bag give you a fright?

KITCHEN HAND:
But uncle, just remember how
your scary tales once took away my breath.
It's no surprise that now
the forest frightens me to death.

GAMEKEEPER:
I know I chatter a good deal.
Sometimes I lay it on a little thick,
but now come on, get real,

vyzvěděti odpověď,
vzmuž se, hej, zaklepej,
na radu se babky ptej!

KUCHTÍK:
Já bych jistě breptal,
jakou úzkost mám –
abys tedy zeptal
se jí na to sám!

HAJNÝ:
Styděl bych se, styděl,
já být otcem tvým!
Ale abys viděl,
že se nebojím:
Ježibabo, hola, hola!

JEŽIBABA – *vyjde z chalupy*:
Kdo to hlučí? Kdo to volá?

Kuchtík se skrývá za hajného.

HAJNÝ:
Stará Háta k tobě posílá,
abys, Ježibabo, radila!

JEŽIBABA:
Za tu radu, za rozumu špetku,
tohle vyžle posílá mi k snědku?
    Sáhne na kuchtíka.
Jen co vykrmí se, chudinka,
bude z něho křehká pečínka!

you have to find an answer quick,
so brace yourself and don't think twice.
just ask the witch for her advice.

KITCHEN HAND:
I'm bound to um and er;
I'm such a bag of nerves I dread
to go, so I'd prefer
if you would ask instead.

GAMEKEEPER:
I would not want a son
so keen to cut and run,
but so that you can see
nothing worries me –
Hey, Ježibaba, come on out!

JEŽIBABA – *emerging from her cottage*:
Who's that shouting? What's it about?

   The kitchen hand hides behind the gamekeeper.

GAMEKEEPER:
Old Hattie sends us here to you
to ask advice – what should we do?

JEŽIBABA:
For that advice, some native wit,
she sends me this puny titbit?
   She touches the kitchen hand.
He needs some fattening up, I'd say,
to make a tender roast one day.

KUCHTÍK – *se zoufale brání*:
Honem, honem, z prokletých těch míst!
Strýčku, strýčku, ona mě chce sníst!

JEŽIBABA – *se chechtá*:
I ty malý zmetku,
hloupé stvoření,
to bych měla k snědku,
čistou pečeni!
Pro peklo ať roste prokletý rod váš –
a teď pověz honem, co mi říci máš!

KUCHTÍK – *s úzkostí*:
Náš princ těžce stůně, převelice –
uhranula jeho srdce jakás kouzelnice!
Přiveď si ji na hrad, vše jí dal,
jako vlastní život vám ji miloval.
Jeho ženou byla by se stala,
ale krásná kouzelnice svatby nedočkala.
Prince když už zmátla docela,
nevěrná ta kouzelnice zmizela.
Celý hrad je kouzlem zmámen podnes –
ďábel sám tu kouzelnici do pekla si odnes'!

VODNÍK – *se vynoří rázem z jezera*:
Kdo že ji odnes'? Koho že zradila?
Hanebné plémě, jež vás sem posílá,
tvorové bídní, prolhaná havěti –
on sám ji zradil, uvrh' ji v prokletí!

HAJNÝ – *na útěku*:
Hastrman! Hastrman!

KITCHEN HAND – *desperately protesting*:
Let's go, let's go – a curse dwells here!
She wants to eat me up, I fear!

JEŽIBABA – *laughing*:
You little freak of nature,
such a silly creature.
Not much to feast on there!
That roast is pretty bare!
May your damned race end up in Hell!
Now tell me quick, what have you got to tell?

KITCHEN HAND – *in trepidation*:
Our prince is ill; it's very serious.
His heart's bewitched by a sorceress.
He brought her to the castle, treated her well.
He loved her just as much as his own life.
She would have then become his wife;
but the fair sorceress, she did not stay;
once the prince had fallen under her spell,
the unfaithful witch then flitted away.
The castle's all still smitten by her spell –
The devil's dragged that beauty off to Hell.

SPIRIT OF THE LAKE – *suddenly emerging
on the surface of the lake*:
Who's taken her, and whom did she betray?
Shame on the tribe that sends you here to us!
There is no truth in what you bad lot say –
he betrayed her and brought on her a curse!

GAMEKEEPER – *beating a fast retreat*:
Water Spirit! Water Spirit!

KUCHTÍK – *za ním*:
Strýčku! Strýčku! Proboha, strýčku!

Utekli.

VODNÍK – *příšerným hlasem*:
Pomstím se, pomstím, kam říš má dosahá!

JEŽIBABA – *belhajíc zpátky do chalupy*:
Hahaha! Hahaha! Hahaha!

Zatím zhasly červánky na západě,
setmělo se, a záhy vyjde měsíc.
Na palouku se sbíhají lesní žínky.

LESNÍ ŽÍNKA – *tančíc*:
Mám, mám, zlaté vlásky mám,
svatojánské mušky slétají se k nim,
ruka moje bílá vlásky rozpustila,
měsíček je češe svitem stříbrným.

JINÁ ŽÍNKA – *tančíc*:
Mám, mám, bílé nožky mám,
proběhla jsem palouk celičký,
proběhla jsem bosa, umyla je rosa,
měsíček je obul v zlaté střevíčky.

TŘETÍ ŽÍNKA – *tančíc*:
Mám, mám, krásné tílko mám,
na palouku v noci svítí jeho vděk.
Kudy běžím všudy, moje bílé údy
do stříbra a zlata šatí měsíček.

KITCHEN HAND – *following him*:
Uncle! Uncle! For goodness sake, uncle!

They run away.

SPIRIT OF THE LAKE – *in a terrifying tone of voice*:
I'll seek revenge, revenge, throughout my realm!

JEŽIBABA – *hobbling off to her cottage*:
Ha, ha, ha! Ha, ha, ha! Ha, ha, ha!

*The red rays of sunset in the west have meanwhile faded
away. Darkness falls and shortly the moon emerges.
The wood nymphs come running, gathering in the glade.*

A WOOD NYMPH – *dancing*:
Mine, mine, soft golden hair, all mine,
attracts fireflies, it draws them all.
From my pale hands the tresses fall,
caressed by silvery light from the moon.

SECOND WOOD NYMPH – *dancing*:
Mine, mine, tiny light feet, all mine,
across the lakeside glade I flew,
bare feet refreshed by evening dew,
moonbeams for slippers, golden, fine.

THIRD WOOD NYMPH – *dancing*:
Mine, mine, fair dainty body, all mine.
By night it elegantly gleams,
as I run free, my alabaster limbs
are swathed in silver-gold moonshine.

LESNÍ ŽÍNKY – *navzájem*:
Dokola, sestřičky, dokola,
v lehounký noční vánek,
za chvíli z rákosí zavolá
zelený hastrmánek.
  Vidouce vodníka:

Už tu je, už tu je,
už si sítě zpravuje,
Hastrmánku, hejahej,
honem si nás nachytej!
Kterou chytíš, mužíčku,
dá ti pěknou hubičku!
Ale žena, hahaha,
za uši ti vytahá!

VODNÍK – *smutně*:
Nelaškujte plaše,
děti moje zlatovlasé,
rodná voda naše
lidským rmutem zkalila se.

LESNÍ ŽÍNKY – *stanou*:
Cože nám ruší veselý rej?
Povídej, mužíčku, povídej!

VODNÍK:
Hluboko na dně sténá
sestrami zavržená
ubohá rusalka bledá!
Běda! Ó běda! Ó běda!
  Ponoří se do jezera.

THE WOOD NYMPHS – *in unison*:
Dance round and round, dear sisters all,
in gentle evening breeze.
Green Water Spirit soon will call
from down amongst the reeds.
  They see Spirit of the Lake.

Here he is, now he's here,
mending his nets — old dear!
Water Spirit, ha, ha, ha!
come on, catch us if you can!
The one you catch, dear man,
will kiss you, kiss you, ooh la la,
But then your wife, ha! ha! ha!
she'll box your ears, ha! ha! ha!

SPIRIT OF THE LAKE – *sadly*:
Don't gaily frolic on tiptoes,
my golden-haired young daughters,
our home in native waters
is defiled by human woes.

THE WOOD NYMPHS – *coming to a standstill*:
What is it spoils our happy play today?
Tell us, kind mannikin, what can you say?

SPIRIT OF THE LAKE:
Poor pale Rusalka's wailing in despair,
deep in the lake, down there.
Her sister nymphs don't want to know.
O woe! O woe! O woe!
  He submerges in the lake.

LESNÍ ŽÍNKA:
Cítím slzu ve zraku,
chlad mne náhle ovál!

Měsíc zajde v mraky.

JINÁ ŽÍNKA:
Do šedivých oblaků
měsíček se schoval!

TŘETÍ ŽÍNKA:
Tma se tiskne v skráně mé –
sestry, sestry, prchněme!

Rozprchnou se.

PRINC – *vyběhne pomaten z lesa*:
Bílá moje lani! Bílá moje lani!
Pohádko! Němý přelude!
Mému naříkání, spěchu bez ustání
konec už nikdy nebude?
Ode dne ke dni touhou štván
hledám tě v lesích udýchán,
noc-li se blíží, tuším tě v ní,
chytám tě v mlze měsíční,
hledám tě širé po zemi —
pohádko, pohádko, vrať se mi!
    Stane.
Tady to bylo! Mluvte, němé lesy!
Vidino sladká, milenko má, kde jsi?
Při všem, co v mrtvém srdci mám,
nebe i zemi zaklínám,
zaklínám Boha i běsy –
ozvi se, ozvi se, kde jsi!

A WOOD NYMPH:
My eyes are filled with tears,
I feel at once a chilly shroud.

The moon disappears behind the clouds.

SECOND WOOD NYMPH:
The kindly moon now disappears
behind a dark grey cloud.

THIRD WOOD NYMPH:
I sense dark thoughts oppressing me.
Sisters, sisters, let us flee!

They scatter.

PRINCE – *runs out of the forest, confused*:
O my white doe! O my white doe!
My fairy tale! Mute vision, white as snow!
Will never more be granted any rest
from my laments, my ceaseless quest?
My yearning day by day still drives me on.
I seek you breathless in those forests yon.
When nightfall comes I sense your presence near.
In moonlit mist I reach out for your hand.
I seek you everywhere throughout the land.
Fairy tale, fairy tale, return, my dear!
   He stops.
This is the place! Mute forests, speak!
Sweet vision, my love, where are you, kept apart?
By all that still remains in my dead heart,
a curse on heaven and earth alike,
a curse on God and all the devils too!
Speak out, speak out, o where are you?

Měsíc vyjde z mraků.

RUSALKA – *se zjeví v měsíčním svitu nad jezerem:*
Miláčku, znáš mne, znáš?
Miláčku, ještě vzpomínáš?

PRINC – *užasne*:
Mrtva-lis dávno, znič mne vráz,
živa-lis ještě, spas mě, spas!

RUSALKA:
Živa ni mrtva, žena ni víla,
prokleta bloudím mátohou!
Marně jsem chvíli v loktech tvých snila
lásku svou, lásku ubohou,
milenkou tvojí kdysi jsem byla –
ale teď jsem jen smrtí tvou!

PRINC:
Bez tebe nelze nikde žít,
můžeš mi, můžeš odpustit?

RUSALKA:
Proč volal jsi mě v náruč svou,
proč ústa tvoje lhala?
Teď měsíční jsem vidinou,
v tvá muka neskonalá.
Teď tebe šálím v nočních tmách,
je zneuctěn můj klín,
a s bludičkami na vodách
tě svedu do hlubin.
Tys hledal vášeň, vím to, vím,
jíž já jsem neměla,
a teď-li tebe políbím,
jsi ztracen docela.

The moon emerges from the clouds.

RUSALKA – *appears above the lake in the light of the moon:*
My love, do you know me, I wonder?
My love, do you still remember?

PRINCE – *in astonishment*:
If you're long dead, destroy me now!
If you still live, save me somehow!

RUSALKA:
Neither alive nor dead, woman nor nymph,
condemned to roam as a phantom wraith
when briefly in your arms I dreamt again
of love — the wretched love I sought in vain.
Once I could give you love, plight my troth,
now all I bring to you is death.

PRINCE:
Without you I cannot live,
can you, can you still forgive?

RUSALKA:
Why did you take me, hold me tight?
Why did your lips have to lie?
I'm but a vision in the moonlight
that will torment you for ever and aye.
As darkness falls, I lure you back
a will o' the wisp above the lake,
my honour lost, at night I may not sleep,
condemned to draw you down into the deep.
You sought a passion, I know, I know,
you sought a passion I could not show,
and if I kiss you now, nought could be worse –
you're cursed, for ever cursed.

Princ se k ní potácí.

PRINC:
Nechci se vrátit v světa rej,
líbej mne, líbej, mír mi přej,
do smrti třeba mě ulíbej!

RUSALKA:
A tys mi tolik, tolik dal,
proč jsi mě, hochu můj, oklamal?

PRINC:
Všechno chci, všechno ti zas dát,
líbej mě, líbej tisíckrát!

RUSALKA – *rozpíná náručí*:
Zda to víš, hochu, zda to víš,
z loktů mých že se nevrátíš,
zkázou to v loktech mých zaplatíš?

PRINC – *vrhne se v její náručí*:
Nechci se vrátit, zemru rád,
nemyslím, nemyslím na návrat!

RUSALKA – *jej obejme a líbá*:
Láska má zmrazí všechen cit,
musím tě v lednou náruč vzít,
musím tě, musím zahubit!

PRINC:
Polibky tvoje hřích můj posvětí!
Umírám šťasten ve tvém objetí!
    Zemře.

The prince staggers towards her.

PRINCE:
Kiss me, kiss me, grant me peace,
let worldly joys for ever cease.
Kiss me to death, kiss me please.

RUSALKA:
I gained so much, so much from you,
o love of mine, why did you not stay true?

PRINCE:
All shall be yours again to have and hold.
Kiss me, kiss me a thousand-fold!

RUSALKA – *with open arms*:
Know you, my love, my dearest one,
from my embrace you never can return?
For in my arms through death you must atone.

PRINCE – *throwing himself into her arms*:
I never will return, happy will I die.
All thoughts of my return I now deny.

RUSALKA – *embracing and kissing him*:
My love will turn all feelings into ice,
I'll hold you now, in my freezing embrace,
I must put you to death, I must, alas!

PRINCE:
My sin shall be absolved by your kiss.
Happy I die, held in your embrace!
   He dies.

VODNÍK – *hluboko pod vodou*:
Nadarmo v loktech zemře ti,
marny jsou všechny oběti,
ubohá rusalko bledá!
Běda! Ó běda! Ó, běda!

RUSALKA – *políbí naposled mrtvého prince*:
Za tvou lásku, za tu krásu tvou,
za tvou lidskou vášeň nestálou,
za všechno, čím klet jest osud můj,
lidská duše, Bůh tě pomiluj!
　　Ponoří se do jezera.

KONEC POHÁDKY

SPIRIT OF THE LAKE – *deep below the surface of the water*:
Held in your arms, he'll die in vain,
all sacrifices nought but pain!
Poor Rusalka, so pale, oh woe!
O woe! O woe! O woe!

RUSALKA – *kissing the dead prince for the last time:*
For your love and for your beauty,
for your human passion's elusive state,
for all the curses that resolved my fate –
upon your human soul God have mercy!
    She submerges in the lake.

END OF THE FAIRY TALE

RUSALKA: A FAIRY TALE IN REVERSE

Once upon a time – and darkness will prevail...
for so the story runs, in every fairy tale.[1]

The opera *Rusalka*, op. 114 (B. 203), by the composer Antonín Dvořák (1841–1904), a setting of the present text, and the last but one of his operas, was composed in 1900. First performed in Prague the following year, it rapidly became not only the best-known of the composer's operas, but the most popular of all Czech operas after Smetana's *The Bartered Bride.*[2] Its place in the standard operatic repertory is securely established today, although it took time before its great beauty and dramatic mastery were fully recognized internationally.

Its libretto, by the author Jaroslav Kvapil (1868–1950), here given a lovely translation by Patrick John Corness, is also a remarkable literary work in its own right. Kvapil called it a 'lyrical fairy tale'; however, this 'fairy tale' has distinctive *fin-de-siècle* features, which will be discussed below by comparison with other works by Kvapil, and which may justify the notion that it is virtually a fairy tale in reverse.

The genesis of the work

After the success of the opera, Kvapil claimed that he had written the libretto in the autumn of 1899, 'without knowing for whom.' He had spent that summer on the Danish island of Bornholm, immersed in the *Folk Tales and Legends* of Božena Němcová and K. J. Erben's *Kytice* (both among the best-known classics of Czech mid-nineteenth-century Romantic literature),[3] and while writing he had also had Hans Christian Andersen's prose fairy tale, "The Little Mermaid," in mind.[4] He had then shown the result to the composers Oskar Nedbal, Karel Kovařovic, Josef Bohuslav Foerster, and Josef Suk, all of whom had shown 'only a friendly interest and no more,' and he had finally 'dared' to approach Dvořák, a well-established figure from the older generation, using František Šubert, the director of the National Theatre, as a go-between, after reading in the papers that the composer was looking for a libretto.[5]

In fact, this account was selective. In 1897, Kvapil had already been made aware by Šubert himself of Dvořák's potential interest in 'a libretto for an opera with a Czech fairy-tale plot.'[6] In any case, Dvořák had already had his interest in Slavonic folklore and fairytales rekindled in 1884, when he had set *Svatební košile* [The wedding shirts], one of the literary reworkings of Czech supernatural legends in Erben's *Kytice*, as an extended cantata for the Birmingham Festival in England. (Under the title *The Spectre's Bride*, it was performed there the following year.) And in the 1890s he had been working on further projects for works based on poems from *Kytice*. Four of these came to fruition in the well-known symphonic poems he composed in 1896,[7] works whose dramatic and musical characteristics anticipate those of his two late fairy-tale operas, *Čert a Káča* [*The Devil and Kate*], premiered in 1899, and *Rusalka*, though the symphonic poems are untexted.[8]

It is unsurprising, then, that Dvořák should have thought of following these works with a full-length opera in the same spirit, or that he should have worked quickly and enthusiastically on *Rusalka* once Kvapil had offered it to him with Šubert's recommendation. But there were complications before this could happen. Kvapil had not responded to Šubert's suggestion immediately in 1897, and by 1899, after he had completed the libretto, he was evidently being pestered for it by a minor Czech composer, Alois Jiránek (1858–1950), based at the time at Kharkiv in Ukraine. In a letter to J. B. Foerster, Kvapil admitted that he felt 'too satisfied with the work to give it away to an uncertain address for a few gulden,'[9] and had to overcome his embarrassment at bypassing Jiránek. However, once he had silenced his conscience to his own satisfaction, and approached Dvořák, it seems that composer and librettist worked in close discussion in face-to-face meetings. Kvapil recalled that Dvořák accepted his text virtually as it stood, apart from requesting some minor changes, such as the addition of Rusalka's aria 'Staletá moudrost tvá všechno ví' at her first encounter with Ježibaba in Act I. Kvapil recalled receiving visits from the train-spotting, and absent-minded, composer 'shortly after seven in the morning (after the composer had been inspecting the locomotives in Prague's various railway stations)'.[10]

Dvořák seems also to have been influenced, in setting the libretto, by the nature of the voice of the distinguished soprano Růžena Maturová, who was a personal friend of Kvapil's wife, the actress Hana Kvapilová (née Kubešová, 1860–1907). Maturová had taken leading operatic roles in the National Theatre since 1893, and took the title role in the premiere of *Rusalka* in 1901. Karel Kovařovic, who was conducting, had wished her to sing the role of the Foreign Princess, but was overruled by Dvořák; Maturová later claimed that the role, and in particular the celebrated 'Song to the Moon' in Act I, had been composed especially for her.[11] After the success of *Rusalka*, Kvapil recalled that Dvořák immediately demanded another libretto to provide Maturová with a new leading role; although he could not fulfil the request, she did sing the leading role in Dvořák's *Armida* in 1904.

Kvapil's work leading up to *Rusalka*

During the 1890s, Kvapil's own career had also been moving progressively in the direction of *Rusalka*, as Dvořák will have known, and *Rusalka* is arguably best read in the light of his previous work. Kvapil had published collections of poetry in the late 1880s, while still a student, which combined the technical polish of Jaroslav Vrchlický (1853–1912) with themes and imagery indebted to Decadence. His interest in the theatre, and a partial turn away from Decadence, had been stimulated after 1890, when he met Hana Kubešová, already mentioned, marrying her in 1894, and from 1891 he began writing reviews of literature and theatre for the daily paper *Hlas národa*.

In 1887 Kubešová had played the emancipated young teacher Petra Stockmann in Pavel Švanda's production of Ibsen's *An Enemy of the People* in his Smíchov theatre in Prague.[12] And it was for Kubešová that Kvapil wrote his Ibsenesque realistic social drama *Bludička* [Will-o'-the-Wisp] in 1896,[13] and then the verse 'fairy tale' *Princezna Pampeliška* [Princess Dandelion] in 1897, both of which foreshadow *Rusalka* in different ways, and illustrate Kvapil's distinctive *fin-de-siècle* representation of female protagonists. (In both of these she played the principal female roles.) Like *Rusalka*, these are framed in terms of a tragic conflict between incompatible worlds, drawing on what had by then become a Romantic cliché – often represented in drama as a fatal conflict between a natural world and a supernatural world, as in Richard Wagner's *Flying Dutchman* of 1843.

In *Bludička*, a drama set in contemporary 1890s Prague, the artist Kamilo Dušek brutally breaks off his six-year liaison with a milliner's assistant, Stáza Faltysová, and abandons the easy-going world of his bohemian friends and colleagues, in order to reinvent himself in the salon world of the *haute bourgeoisie* of Prague, and to court the rich Helena Lindnerová. Among the cynical, and in reality philistine, Prague bourgeois, Dušek is out of his depth as a parvenu; his vocation as an artist is corrupted, and the 'will-o'-the-wisp' of their world ultimately brings him to suicide. But it is Lindnerová who is the central character. She is a cynical free-thinker, critical of the hypocritical double standard in sexual matters maintained by conventional society. As she says to her lover, Dr. Vlasák, in Act III, 'society would noisily laugh you to scorn if you claimed you were entering marriage as pure as you men expect a woman to be, and it will noisily hold you in contempt if you oppose its pharisaism. I am too independent not to claim that right for myself as well.'[14] In depicting an Ibsenesque woman calling for equality in such matters, Kvapil was not only providing his wife with a congenial part to play, but also flirting with contemporary feminism; this will be addressed below.

Significantly, however, Kvapil's play finally offers no escape for a woman, even one demanding equality, from the pharisaism of contemporary society.

In the following year, Kvapil turned to representing incompatible worlds through an invented legend, in a verse 'fairy tale' of great beauty, *Princezna Pampeliška*.[15] This quasi-symbolist play owes nothing to the contemporary symbolism of Maurice Maeterlinck's *Pelléas et Mélisande* (1893), but in some ways resembles Gerhart Hauptmann's *Die versunkene Glocke* [The sunken bell], also a verse fairy tale, which appeared in 1896.[16] *Princezna Pampeliška* was a five-act drama, provided with incidental music by the composer Josef Bohuslav Foerster, and immediately became a popular success. The variety of its verse prefigures that of *Rusalka* in some ways: both include a wide range of contrasted metres and registers of language for the sake of characterization, using a variety of verse structures resembling those of the literary folk-legends of Erben's *Kytice*.[17] Both also include folk-like songs or dances, with rhymed texts, effectively as separate numbers, as well as episodes providing comic relief. Princess Pampeliška herself is another independently-minded woman. She begins Act I with an outright rejection of the arranged marriage with a 'mighty prince of Hispania' that her father has set up for her. She escapes from the palace to become a homeless tramp, together with *hloupý Honza* ('stupid Johnny,' a stock simple-Simon folk Czech figure), who is a good-hearted peasant boy she meets along the way. However, 'darkness will prevail,' for this is a fairy tale in Kvapil's mould: Pampeliška cannot enjoy the happy-ever-after life with Honza that would normally be expected from the genre. Her fate is symbolized in her name, 'Pampeliška' ('Dandelion'). Just as a golden dandelion flower lasts only as long as the sun is shining upon it, and quickly fades, so she too wastes away, and her golden hair turns grey, as summer turns to autumn, and the sky turns dark. Finally, she is blown away on the wind without trace, like dandelion fluff.

In this fairy tale, then, the normal pattern of the genre is significantly reversed. Not only does it lack the happy end that might be expected, but the final tragedy becomes absolute. The female protagonist is completely annihilated, and for no clear reason, other than the supposed laws of nature – not even for her temerity in breaking free from her father's wishes and his authority.

Rusalka: Another reversed fairy tale

Rusalka, another three-act 'fairy tale,' continues the pattern of the reversed fairy tale, which had been established in Princezna Pampeliška, with a female protagonist who rejects her predestined status. As an opera libretto Rusalka might be expected to be more trivial, from a literary point of view, than the previous drama, but, paradoxically, the reverse seems true, and indeed Kvapil hoped that Rusalka would stand up as a literary work of art in its own right.[18] While traditional Czech folk motifs are deployed in Princezna Pampeliška to produce a rather original and slightly diffuse plot, a simplified and unified plot is peopled in Rusalka, by contrast, with characters and narrative elements familiar from the literature.

Rather than 'adapting' any existing narrative, Kvapil selects varied narrative 'echoes,' as he calls them in his introduction to the published libretto, from diverse intertexts, weaving them together to cast ironic light on one another.[19] Those he lists are Friedrich de la Motte Fouqué's novel, Undine (1811); Hans Christian Andersen's prose tale "The Little Mermaid" (1837); the medieval French Mélusine legends; Václav Kliment Klicpera's play, The Czech Melusine (1848);[20] Gerhart Hauptmann's verse play, Die versunkene Glocke, (1896); and the poems 'The Lily', 'The Water Goblin' and 'The Golden Spinning-Wheel' drawn from the two editions of Erben's Kytice.

Some of these, entirely rewritten, supply characters for Rusalka. Besides the title role herself, who will be discussed further below, two central examples are the Spirit of the Lake and Ježibaba, who unexpectedly become brother and sister. Kvapil's Spirit of the Lake is Rusalka's father, an absolute ruler who presides over his realm, more or less benignly, and is consumed with sorrow at Rusalka's fate. His kingdom is a nocturnal, marine parallel to the sunny Arcadia of pastoral: as ironically depicted at the beginning of Act I, it is a carefree, unproblematic kingdom of song and dance, in which sex is apparently constantly available and responsible fidelity laughingly unknown. He differs in most respects from his threatening, malignant counterparts in Kvapil's alleged models, who include Fouqué's Kühleborn (Undine's uncle in that tale, an uncontrollable 'elemental spirit' of lakes, streams and wells), Hauptmann's ominous Nickelmann, and Erben's Vodník (the bloodthirsty water-spirit who abducts an anonymous girl as his wife, and finally kills her child). He is altogether more akin to the king, father of Princess Pampeliška, of Kvapil's other fairy tale, who is also essentially good-hearted, though comically feckless, but must also suffer the rebellion of his daughter against his quasi-feudal authority.

Likewise, Kvapil's witch Ježibaba, whose name was stolen from the Czech translation of 'Wittichen,' her counterpart in Hauptmann's play, is Rusalka's elderly, formidable, and partly comic aunt, who helps Rusalka to escape her father's realm at the cost of losing her voice. Ježibaba has a down-to-earth, unsentimental attitude to the younger generation and its absurd infatuations, and she is feared by the comical 'rude mechanicals' of Act II, but she is ultimately indulgent to Rusalka and her troubles, even though her final advice, that Rusalka should use the knife against her faithless prince, is brutal. She is a wonderful invention, borrowed from her counterpart in Andersen's "Little Mermaid." But Andersen's witch is weaker than Kvapil's. Andersen has her converting his mermaid's tail into legs, and cutting out her tongue, and these processes, involving permanent pain, bleeding, and silent suffering, bear no real connection with the prince's infidelity. Moreover, Andersen's witch dilutes and weakens the final devastating tragedy of the tale by arbitrarily, and sentimentally, changing the rules of the game at the last moment.[21]

The reciprocal roles of Ježibaba and Rusalka in the drama have been well characterized by the German theatre director Jürgen Schläder in a provocative article from 1981 seeking to reinterpret the opera in Symbolist terms.[22] Schläder points out that the two encounters between Rusalka and Ježibaba, symmetrically placed within the opera, are crucial to it. They dramatize Rusalka's two central decisions – in Act I, to abandon her life as a water nymph, and, in Act III, to reverse that decision. (The centrality of Ježibaba seems to have been realized by Dvořák, in his request for additional text for Rusalka for her dialogue with Ježibaba in Act I, already mentioned above.) Schläder argued, rightly or wrongly, that these two decisions, and especially Rusalka's final choice to cast the knife away though she knows she faces annihilation in doing so, make her a 'psychologically complex character' rather than a traditional fairy-tale figure.[23] And his suggestion has been taken still further by the Dvořák scholar Jarmila Gabrielová, who has interpreted the opera as a 'drama of human, indeed women's, emancipation,'[24] in which Rusalka's final decision is one in which she achieves true freedom at last by fully embracing the tragedy of human existence.

Such suggestions highlight the ambiguities of interpretation that are possible with this work and its final tragedy, and they are highlighted by Dvořák's setting of the final scene. The music swells to a triumphant crescendo, in a self-quotation from the composer's second symphony op. 4 (B.12), of 1865, revised in 1887.[25] It amounts to a powerful, and paradoxical, celebration of Rusalka's final annihilation, even though no union with her prince is in prospect, even in an afterlife, as Schläder rightly points out, and no reprieve is possible.

All three of Kvapil's dramas considered here (*Bludička*, *Princezna Pampeliška*, and *Rusalka*), and especially the reversed fairy tales of the latter two, stage brave women who reject constraints placed upon them by family or society.

Their gestures towards emancipation, and in part towards gender equality, are all powerful. Yet in all three cases, the rebellion of these women is pessimistically and tragically doomed to complete failure – 'for so the story runs, in every fairy tale.' One can hardly ignore the resonance that all three dramas would have had in their own period, when the 'women's question' was a subject of lively debate in Bohemia, where women's suffrage would soon be established (around 1920, indeed more quickly, and with less opposition, than in English-speaking countries). In particular, the gender politics of the future president of independent Czechoslovakia, Tomáš Garrigue Masaryk (1850–1937), deserves notice, not least because Kvapil was himself to enter politics and to become a parliamentarian in Masaryk's government in later years. Possibly under the influence of his Unitarian American wife Charlotte, Masaryk himself was consistently in favour of women's equality, especially in education, and a vociferous opponent of the double standard in sexual behaviour between men and women.[26]

It must immediately be said that these pessimistic dramas are in no way mechanical representations of Masaryk's policies, not least because Masaryk himself rejected pessimism and decadence in politics, and it may be that Kvapil at the turn of the century is still permitting himself a partially decadent world in which utter pessimism is legitimate. Yet the representation of women's aspirations that is evident in them is perhaps a realistic reflection of what was possible in the liberation of women in Bohemia at the turn of the century. It is particularly ironic that Kvapil's final turn to a 'fairy tale' offers us, not an optimistic turn to a more humane and egalitarian society, in which women take their rightful and equal place – for this is what one might legitimately expect from the genre, and this is what Masaryk stood for – but its complete negation: the opening of a modernist abyss. He turns the genre on its head. And the piece is all the more powerful as a result. For a modern opera-going public, and for a modern readership of

Kvapil's poetry, the work remains a heart-rending dramatization of the frustration and negation of the legitimate aspirations of the human heart.

Geoffrey Chew
Egham, April–May 2020

1) Jaroslav Kvapil, *Princezna Pampeliška: pohádka* (Prague: F. Šimáček, 1897), from the Nurse's Prologue:
> Bylo nebylo – a všechno zmizí v tmách...
> Ale to se děje ve všech pohádkách!

2) The opera immediately received a blisteringly hostile review (Zdeněk Nejedlý, 'Dvořákova Rusalka,' *Rozhledy* 11, no. 8 (25 May 1901) 205), which contributed to a lengthy controversy pitting a 'conservative' Dvořák against an anachronistically idealized 'modernist' Smetana. With this review, Nejedlý (later a prominent politician, and an ideologue of Stalinism) launched his career as a writer on music, alleging that *Rusalka* was anti-national and un-Czech, and that it did not pass muster when judged according to Wagnerian principles. The extensive ramifications of the ensuing debate cannot be discussed here; for details, see the exemplary discussion in Brian S. Locke, *Opera and Ideology in Prague*, Eastman Studies in Music (Rochester: University of Rochester Press, 2006) 36–43.

3) Božena Němcová, *Národní báchorky a pověsti* [National folk tales and legends], 7 volumes (Prague: Jaroslav Pospíšil, 1845-8; 2nd enlarged ed., 1854-5); Karel Jaromír Erben, *Kytice z pověstí národních* [A bouquet of national legends] (Prague: Jaroslav Pospíšil, 1853; 2nd ed., Prague: Jaroslav Pospíšil, 1861).

4) Hans Christian Andersen, 'Den lille Havfrue' [The little mermaid], in his *Eventyr, fortalt for Børn* [Fairy tales, told for children] (Copenhagen: C. A. Reitzel, 1837).

5) Jaroslav Kvapil, 'O vzniku Rusalky,' *Hudební revue* 4 (1911) 428-30, and Kvapil's brief introduction to the published libretto. Kvapil's accounts are summarized in Otakar Šourek, *Život a dílo Antonína Dvořáka* 4 (Prague: Hudební matice Umělecké besedy, 1933) 107-14, and in much subsequent literature, including Ivan Vojtěch, 'Rusalka,' in *Pipers Enzyklopädie des Musiktheaters: Oper, Operette, Musical, Ballett*, 2 (Munich: Piper, 1987) 101-6.

6) Markéta Hallová, '*Rusalka* and its Librettist, Jaroslav Kvapil: Some New Discoveries,' in *Rethinking Dvořák: Views from Five Countries*, ed. David R.

Beveridge (Oxford: Clarendon Press, 1996) 107–13 (this quotation at p. 108). On the composer's interest in other types of plot at this time, cf. David R. Beveridge, 'A Rare Meeting of Minds in Kvapil's and Dvořák's *Rusalka*: The Background, the Artistic Result, and Response by the World of Opera,' in *Czech Music Around 1900*, ed. Lenka Křupková and Jiří Kopecký (Hillsdale: Pendragon Press, 2017) 61–80, here p. 63. Kvapil was still referring back to a 'time when I was writing the text of *Rusalka*, without knowing for whom' in a tribute to Růžena Maturová, the 'first Rusalka,' undated, but after the death of his wife in 1907, quoted in Artuš Rektorys, *Růžena Maturová* (Prague: O. Girgal, 1936) 47–8.

7) 'Vodník' [The water-goblin] op. 107, 'Polednice' [The noonday witch] op. 108, 'Zlatý kolovrat' [The golden spinning-wheel] op. 109, and 'Holoubek' [The wild dove] op. 110. For an interpretation of these, and of the 'Píseň bohatýrská' [Heroic song] op. 111 that followed them in 1897, as 'proto-operas,' see Clare A. Thornley, *'Dramas without a Stage, Acts without Singers':* *Rethinking the Symphonic Poems of Antonín Dvořák* (doctoral dissertation, New York University, 2011).

8) Jan Smaczny, 'Dvořák: The Operas,' *Dvořák and his World*, ed. Michael B. Beckerman (Princeton: Princeton UP, 1993) 127.

9) Jaroslav Kvapil, letter to Josef Bohuslav Foerster of 30 September 1899, here quoted from Hallová, *'Rusalka* and its Librettist' (n. 6) 109.

10) These details, from Jaroslav Kvapil, 'O vzniku Rusalky' (n. 5) 428–9, and letters concerning *Rusalka* from Dvořák to Kvapil sent from Vysoká near Příbram, are reprinted in Otakar Šourek, ed., *Dvořák ve vzpomínkách a dopisech*, 2nd ed. (Prague: Topičova edice, 1938) 165–70.

11) See Artuš Rektorys, *Růžena Maturová* (n. 6) 47–8.

12) See František Černý, 'Potomstvo se bude musit učit jeho jméno zpaměti', *Ipse ipsa Ibsen: sborník ibsenových studií*, ed. Karolina Stehlíková (Soběslav: Nakladatelství Elg, 2006) 18–58, here from pp. 31–2. (The character from the play is misidentified by Černý as 'Pavla' Stockmann.) Ibsen had featured on the Prague stage since a production of his *Pillars of Society* in 1878, as *Podpory společnosti*. I am grateful to Pavel Drábek for making a copy of Stehlíková's book available to me, and for other references and other material.

13) Jaroslav Kvapil, *Bludička: drama o čtyřech dějstvích* (Prague: F. Topič, 1896); *Princezna Pampeliška* (n. 1). See the critiques of these two plays by the influential critic F. X. Šalda, in his 'Jaroslav Kvapil: Bludička,' *Literární listy* 17 (1895–6) 305–9, and 'Jaroslav Kvapil: Princezna Pampeliška,' *Literární listy* 19 (1897–8), reprinted respectively in F. X. Šalda, *Kritické*

projevy 3: 1896–1897, Soubor díla F. X. Šaldy, 12, ed. Karel Dvořák (Prague: Melantrich, 1950) 71–81 and 301–6. There is an English translation of *Bludička*, by Šárka B. Hrbková: 'The Will o' the Wisp: A Drama in Four Acts,' *Poet Lore* 27 (1916) 1–75.

14) Kvapil, *Bludička* (n. 13) 91: 'Společnost by se ti hlasitě vysmála, kdybys řekl, že jdeš do manželství čist, jako vy muži od ženy žádáte – a hlasitě tě zhanobí, vzepřeš-li se jejímu farizejství. Jsem příliš svá, abych téhož práva i pro sebe nepožadovala.'

15) Kvapil, *Princezna Pampeliška* (n. 1).

16) Gerhart Hauptmann, *Die versunkene Glocke: Ein deutsches Märchendrama* (Berlin: S. Fischer, 1897).

17) As for *Rusalka*, Kvapil had the following to say: 'I think it was our love for Erben and the tone of Erben's ballads, which I tried to approach in *Rusalka*, that brought me close to Dvořák; that it spoke more to him than the libretto alone could have done' ['Myslím, že mě s Dvořákem sblížila naše láska k Erbenovi, a tón balad Erbenových, jimž jsem se hleděl "Rusalkou" přiblížit, že pověděl Dvořákovi víc, než mohlo libreto samo'] (from Kvapil, 'O vzniku Rusalky' (n. 5), reprinted in Šourek, ed., *Dvořák ve vzpomínkách a dopisech* (n. 10), 166).

18) 'Rád bych vůbec, aby tato práce moje nebyla pokládána za pouhé libretto k opeře, za pouhou nesamostatnou a literárně lhostejnou odliku jiných děl' (Kvapil, introduction to libretto).

19) Such 'echoes' (*ozvuky*, or *ohlasy*) are a well-known genre of Czech Romantic poetry, ultimately derived from poets such as Byron, Thomas Moore or Robert Burns, usually representing the characteristics of a nation recaptured with difficulty from some golden age: well-known examples are the *Ohlasy písní ruských a českých* [Echoes of Russian and Czech songs] of František Ladislav Čelakovský (Prague: Laichter, 1839).

20) Václav Kliment Klicpera, *Česká Melusina: dramatická národní báchorka w pateru dějstwí* (Prague: Dr J. A. Gabriel, 1848).

21) Further on the pessimism of the close of 'The Little Mermaid,' which was bowdlerized in some German and Czech translations, and its modernist implications, see Helena Březinová, *Slavíci, mořské víly a bolavé zuby: pohádky H. Ch. Andersena mezi romantismem a modernitou* (Brno: Host, 2018) 200–13.

22) Jürgen Schläder, 'Märchenoper oder symbolistisches Musikdrama? Zum Interpretationsrahmen der Titelrolle in Dvořáks "Rusalka"', *Die Musikforschung* 34/1 (1981) 25–39. For another interpretation of *Rusalka* (and of *Bludička*) in terms of a conflict between the culture of the Czech

National Revival and that of cosmopolitan modernism, see my own earlier article: Geoffrey Chew, 'The Rusalka as an Endangered Species: Modernist Aspects and Intertexts of Kvapil's and Dvořák's *Rusalka*', *Hudební věda* 11 (2003) 371–9.

23) Schläder, 'Märchenoper oder symbolistisches Musikdrama?' (n. 22) 29. Coincidentally, this article was quickly followed in 1983 by a celebrated production of the opera for the English National Opera by David Pountney, set in a Victorian or Edwardian nursery, with a nod to the period, and interpreting the plot in psychological terms as the initiation of the pubescent heroine into first love and sexuality. See the comments on this production and this opera in Marina Warner, *From the Beast to the Blonde: On Fairy Tales and their Tellers* (London: Chatto & Windus, 1994) 396–9. Pountney's interpretation established the reputation of the opera in Britain securely for the first time, even though it arguably rides roughshod over some of the narrative, and this production, rightly or wrongly, has encouraged yet more revisionist interpretations in subsequent years.

24) Jarmila Gabrielová, 'Dvořáks und Kvapils *Rusalka* und das Lebensgefühl des fin de siècle,' *Aspekte der Musik, Kunst und Religion zur Zeit der Tschechischen Moderne / Aspects of Music, Arts and Religion during the Period of Czech Modernism*, edited by Aleš Březina and Eva Velická, Martinů-Studien 2 (Bern: Peter Lang, 2009) 67–86: '[Ich verstehe] diese Oper als ein Drama der menschlichen (Frauen!) Emanzipation und des schmerzvollen Weges zum vollwertigen und freien menschlichen Dasein und zugleich als großartiges und hinreißendes Gleichnis oder Metapher des Menschenschicksals.'

25) Symphony No. 2 in B flat, op. 4 (B.12), of 1865, revised in 1887. For details, see Beveridge, 'A Rare Meeting of Minds in Kvapil's and Dvořák's *Rusalka*' (n. 6) 66–70. Beveridge offers a speculative attempt at interpretation in terms of Dvořák's personal life: 'Perhaps the torments of the water nymph Rusalka reminded Dvořák of those he had himself endured in his youth, and of his victory over those torments in the music of his Second Symphony' (70).

26) Examples of Masaryk's later gender politics can be found in his *Mnohoženství a jednoženství: plán pohlavní převýchovy národní* [Polygamy and monogamy: A plan for national sexual re-education] (Prague: B. Kočí, 1925), and his *Moderní názor na ženu: otisk přednášky z roku 1904* [The modern idea of woman: Reprint of a lecture from 1904] (Vyškov: Zemská organisace pokrokových žen moravských, [1930]). For overviews, see Melissa Feinberg, *Elusive Equality: Gender, Citizenship, and the Limits of Democracy*

in Czechoslovakia, 1918-1950, Pitt Series in Russian and East European Studies (Pittsburgh: University of Pittsburgh Press, 2006), especially chap. 1 ('Masaryk, Feminism, and Democracy in the Czech Lands'), and Marie L. Neudorfl, 'Masaryk and the Women's Question,' in *T. G. Masaryk (1850-1937)*, 1 (*Thinker and Politician*), edited by Stanley B. Winters (London: Macmillan Press, 1990) 258–82.

TRANSLATOR'S NOTE[1]

Jaroslav Kvapil's dramatic poem *Rusalka: Lyrická pohádka o třech dějstvích* [The water nymph: A lyrical fairy tale in three acts] is a Czech literary masterpiece deserving the translator's best efforts to offer anglophone readers an experience comparable with that enjoyed by readers of the original work.[2] The challenge is to successfully convey to readers of the English translation the ideo-aesthetic content of Jaroslav Kvapil's work. This involves conveying the true semantic content of the poem, while re-stylizing[3] the source text in a way that achieves functional-stylistic equivalence on a formal level. The most prominent formal aspect of the work is the rhyme. The original is rhymed throughout and, although the English language has at its disposal a far more limited repertoire of rhyme words than Czech – the former is notoriously more limited in this respect than many other languages[4] – the task must be attempted, as it would entail a significant stylistic loss to translate *Rusalka* in non-rhyming verse. My translation strategy here is to derive rhyme words from the semantic content of the source text, finding either direct lexical counterparts or concepts derived from its contextual meaning, wherever possible avoiding recourse to external 'padding,' i.e. words which provide the rhyme but have no justification in terms of semantic content. Rhyme schemes vary between Czech and English; in English versification, recourse may be had to consonance,[5] examples of which in this translation are:

> quite soon inside your home she'll steal
> [...] upon your silver den she'll call

> Then when once more he comes
> and I wind him in my arms,
> he too will hold me close
> with hot passion in his kiss.

The natural rhythm of Czech differs from that of English. In Czech, the dynamic stress is invariably on the first syllable of a word and this contrast with English is compounded by the fact that the duration of Czech vowels often carries meaning; the distinction between long and short vowels is one of semantics rather than emphasis. This means that the rhythm of the Czech source text cannot easily be followed in English translation any more than its phonology; the translator must re-stylize the lines using means of expression natural to English, but ideally achieving a comparable ideo-aesthetic effect overall.

The names of the Czech mythological characters are treated as follows, in order of their appearance. *Lesní žínky* are translated as *Wood Nymphs*, nymphs being in ancient Greek mythology minor goddesses in the form of attractive young women looking after features of nature such as flowers, trees, forests, stretches of water, mountains, etc.

For the *Vodník* I adopt the term *Spirit of the Lake*; he is associated with the lake depicted in the opening scene. In the familiar natural environment of the story's setting, Czech *voda* [water] would be interpreted by a Czech audience or reader as *lake* or *pond*. This interpretation is given in the first translated line: *stojí měsíc nad vodou* [the moon lights up the lake below].[6] Rusalka and Ježibaba are kept as untranslated names, as a 'foreignizing'[7] strategy seems appropriate in these cases. None of the characters in the poem actually has a proper name; the Spirit of the Lake, the Wood Nymphs, the Prince, the Foreign Princess, the Huntsman, the Gamekeeper, and the Kitchen Hand are all generic common nouns. The same applies to the Water Nymph and the Forest Witch, but they are traditionally known by their original Czech names *Rusalka* and *Ježibaba* in English translation. The present translation could not be headed *The Water Nymph* rather than *Rusalka* without dissociating the heroine and the story of the original dramatic poem created by Kvapil's poetic genius from the *Rusalka* of Dvořák's opera familiar today. It seems self-evident that the title of the work and the name of the eponymous central heroine should be the 'foreignizing' *Rusalka*. Logically, *Ježibaba* follows suit.

An important stylistic feature of Czech, particularly prevalent in folklore, is the diminutive. The first word of the aria to the moon – *Měsíčku* – is morphologically significant, carrying much more meaning than the plain denotation *moon*. It is a diminutive form signifying endearment and it is also a form of address (in grammatical terms, the vocative case). This means that from the outset we know that Rusalka is addressing the moon as a sympathetic observer. The nature of the relationship is highlighted by this use of an intimate rather than formal means of address. The functions of these grammatically distinct forms in Czech can be difficult to convey in English, but they are amongst the most prominent stylistic features of Kvapil's lyrical fairy tale[8] and, along with the frequent repetition of these and other expressions, constitute a powerful intensifying element of the composition, further enhanced by Dvořák's musical setting, which exploits them wonderfully.

Aspects of style important for the characterization include polyphony of voices; in particular, the lower style of dialogues between the Gamekeeper and the Kitchen Hand and the idiosyncratic language of the witch *Ježibaba* naturally differ from the frequently elevated style of Rusalka, Spirit of the Lake, the Prince and the Foreign Princess. These features are observed in the translation. For anglophone readers, the incantations of *Ježibaba* are considered more culturally akin to those of the three witches in William Shakespeare's *Macbeth* – an allusion to *Double, double toil and trouble; Fire burn and cauldron bubble* offers an experience closer to that of the original than the *Fee fi fo fum* of the Giant in *Jack and the Beanstalk,* or the *abracadabra* of music-hall magicians.

Patrick John Corness

1) Some of the points mentioned are also discussed in my chapter, "Two English Translations of Jaroslav Kvapil's *Rusalka* libretto," in *Opera and Translation: Eastern and Western Perspectives*, eds. Adriana Şerban and Kelly Kar Yue Chan (Amsterdam: John Benjamins, forthcoming).

2) With literary translation in mind, Jiří Levý writes: "We will not insist that what readers experience through their perception of the original must be identical with what readers experience through their perception of the translation; rather we will insist on functional identity in terms of the respective overall cultural-historical frameworks to which the readers belong." *The Art of Translation*, trans. Patrick Corness, ed. Zuzana Jettmarová (Amsterdam: John Benjamins, 2011) 20.

3) Jiří Levý identifies three stages of the translation process, namely 1) apprehension: deep understanding of the meaning of the source text; 2) interpretation: distinguishing contextual variants of meaning; and 3) re-stylization: conveying the ideo-aesthetic content of the source text through appropriate means of expression in the target language (ibid., 31).

4) Synthetic languages (Russian, Czech and to a certain extent also Italian, German and French) have a far broader repertoire of rhymes than analytical languages (again, English is the purest example) (ibid., 233).

5) Consonance is found, for example, in these lines by Emily Dickinson:

> Father – I bring thee – not myself – That were the little **load** –
> I bring thee the imperial heart
> I had not strength to **hold**
> Your Breath has time to straighten – ,
> Your brain – to bubble **cool** – ,
> Deals One Imperial Thunderbolt
> That scalps your naked **soul** –

The Poems, reading edition, ed. R.W. Franklin (Cambridge: Belknap Press of Harvard UP, 1999) 148.

6) The root morpheme *vod-*, meaning water, occurs in *voda* [water], *nad vodou* [above the water, i.e. lake] and *vodník* [water spirit/spirit of the lake].

7) As Lawrence Venuti puts it, the German philosopher Friedrich Schleiermacher, discussing methods of translation, "allowed the translator to choose between a domesticating practice, an ethnocentric reduction of the foreign text to receiving cultural values, bringing the author back home, and a foreignizing practice, an ethnodeviant pressure on those values to register the linguistic and cultural differences of the foreign text, sending

the reader abroad." *The Translator's Invisibility. A History of Translation.* Second edition (London: Routledge, 2008) 15.

8) Alexandr Stich, "Kvapilova Rusalka jako jazykový, slohový a literární fenomén" [Kvapil's Rusalka as a linguistic, stylistic and literary phenomenon], *Estetika* 29, no. 3 (1992) 11-35.

ABOUT THE TRANSLATOR

Patrick John Corness is a literary translator from Czech, German, Polish, Russian, and Ukrainian. He is currently Visiting Professor of Translation at Coventry University, England, and has undertaken joint research and publications with Charles University in Prague. In 2013 he was awarded the Silver Medal of the Faculty of Arts at Charles University for achievements in the international dissemination of Czech culture and scholarship.

MODERN CZECH CLASSICS

The modern history of Central Europe is notable for its political and cultural discontinuities and often violent changes, as well as its attempts to preserve and (re)invent traditional cultural identities. This series cultivates contemporary translations of influential literary works that have been unavailable to a global readership due to censorship, the effects of the Cold War, and the frequent political disruptions in Czech publishing and its international ties. Readers of English, in today's cosmopolitan Prague and anywhere in the physical and electronic world, can now become acquainted with works that capture the Central European historical experience – works that have helped express and form Czech and Central European identity, humour, and imagination. Believing that any literary canon can be defined only in dialogue with other cultures, the series publishes classics, often used in Western university courses, as well as (re)discoveries aiming to provide new perspectives in the study of literature, history, and culture. All titles are accompanied by an afterword. Translations are reviewed and circulated in the global scholarly community before publication – this is reflected by our nominations for literary awards.

Published titles

Zdeněk Jirotka: *Saturnin* (2003, 2005, 2009, 2013; pb 2016)
Vladislav Vančura: *Summer of Caprice* (2006; pb 2016)
Karel Poláček: *We Were a Handful* (2007; pb 2016)
Bohumil Hrabal: *Pirouettes on a Postage Stamp* (2008)
Karel Michal: *Everyday Spooks* (2008)
Eduard Bass: *The Chattertooth Eleven* (2009)
Jaroslav Hašek: *Behind the Lines: Bugulma and Other Stories* (2012; pb 2016)
Bohumil Hrabal: *Rambling On* (2014; pb 2016)
Ladislav Fuks: *Of Mice and Mooshaber* (2014)
Josef Jedlička: *Midway upon the Journey of Our Life* (2016)
Jaroslav Durych: *God's Rainbow* (2016)
Ladislav Fuks: *The Cremator* (2016)
Bohuslav Reynek: *The Well at Morning* (2017)
Viktor Dyk: *The Pied Piper* (2017)
Jiří R. Pick: *Society for the Prevention of Cruelty to Animals* (2018)
Views from the Inside: Czech Underground Literature and Culture
(1948–1989), ed. M. Machovec (2018)
Ladislav Grosman: *The Shop on Main Street* (2019)
Bohumil Hrabal: *Why I Write? The Early Prose from 1945 to 1952* (2019)
Ludvík Vaculík: *A Czech Dreambook* (2019)
Jiří Pelán: Bohumil Hrabal: *A Full-length Portrait* (2020)

Forthcoming

Jan Procházka: *The Ear*
Ivan Jirous: *The End of the World, Poetry and Prose*
Jan Čep: *Common Rue*
Jiří Weil: *Lamentation for 77,297 Victims*
Vladislav Vančura: *Shares and Swords*
Libuše Moníková: *Verklärte Nacht*